CW01198269

FLOGGING FAITH

A Submissives of Rawhide Ranch Story

ALI WILLIAMS

RAWHIDE RANCH

Published by A&A Publications:
https://authoralliebelle.eo.page/rawhideranch

Cover by AllyCat's Creations

Edited by Maggie Ryan

Formatting by Royalty Writes Enterprises:
https://bit.ly/RoyaltyWritesEnterprises

Faith has no clue how to be a submissive.

She thought she did. She's dedicated years of her life to studying the people and relationships around her, to learning everything she can about the lifestyle she craves.

And yet, over and over again, she is told she's doing it wrong. That she's too forward, too bold, too… everything.

Until her.

Gorgeous, curvy Bex not only tolerates Faith's straightforward ways, she celebrates them, and everything else about her. When Faith surrenders to the sting of Bex's flogger, for the first time she finds the freedom and joy she's always craved from her submission.

But old wounds run deep. Even if Faith can accept Bex's sweet dominance, there's still one last lesson for her to learn:

That there is no wrong way to love…or to be loved.

For Abi. From your rainbow princess…

Please be aware that this story contains references to anxiety, sensory overwhelm and kink (lots of it!). I hope I have treated Faith and Bex's experiences and emotions with the care that they and you deserve.

CHAPTER One

The club was really busy.

Faith sat on the throne—sitting on the throne always gave her a sense of power and naughtiness because brats weren't really supposed to sit there—and looked out across the room.

It wasn't the first time Faith had visited X Rooms; she'd been with a group of friends before, and the small private kink club was well stocked and well laid out.

She still felt out of place though.

The first time she'd visited, she'd ended up supporting her friends more than having any scenes herself. Sitting and watching didn't exactly suit her AuDHD mind, and this time she'd come on her own, thinking perhaps she'd meet someone who'd like to play with her here.

It was Queer Night, which meant she'd had less swaggering male Doms wander over and tell her to get on her knees. As much as she loved submitting, those kind of entitled orders just got her back up.

But none of the women at the club seemed to have any interest in her, and all of her attempts at starting conversation seemed to trail off into nothingness.

Faith was not great at small talk. She just wanted someone to pop her on a cross and flog the living daylights out of her. But apparently being that forthright about what she wanted appeared to turn people off. When she'd said that to one of the Dommes who'd wandered over, she'd cocked an eyebrow and said she wasn't interested in brats who topped from the bottom.

But Faith didn't want to top from the bottom, she just

knew what she wanted, and nothing she'd ever read had told her that wasn't something you were supposed to say.

She looked longingly at the St. Andrew's Cross, and sighed. Maybe next time she'd have better luck.

"Hello," said a voice. She turned and saw a short fat woman, long red hair down to her waist, smiling shyly at her. "I'm Mandi. Are you okay? You seem sad."

"I'm Faith," she replied, and then added, because she didn't want to worry them. "I'm fine thanks."

A taller butch woman in a suit came up behind Mandi and put her hand on the redhead's shoulder. "I'm Amelia. We're not hitting on you, just wanted to see if you were alright."

It was the first time all evening anyone had shown any kindness toward her and Faith found herself welling up.

"Oh no!" Mandi plonked herself on the floor and held out her hands to Faith. "Come sit here and have a cuddle!"

And for some reason, Faith obeyed. Perhaps it was because Mandi gave off the least Domme-y vibes she'd ever come across. She was warm, and soft, and her embrace was just a comfort. It had been a long time since Faith had felt consoled like that.

She didn't let herself cry, not properly, but she rested her head on Mandi's shoulder and took some deep breaths.

"Look," said Amelia. "It seems like you're not having the best time, and we were only visiting because Mandi wanted to see what a kink club was like but didn't want to bump into anyone she knew."

Mandi grinned at Faith. "I'm a Little some of the time, and some Bigs get all weird about Littles in dungeons."

"So, we were probably going to head out soon anyways. Do you want to come with us? We can grab some dinner and have a chat. I'm just a bit worried about leaving you on your own here."

Faith found herself nodding. "I'd have to check in with my friend, though."

"Of course," said Amelia. "And you can send them a photo of our IDs, if that would help?"

It definitely would. Being safe was one of the things Faith had been most nervous about attending X Rooms on her own.

"That sounds nice," she said, her voice nervous. "As long as you don't mind me crashing your date?"

"Not at all," said Mandi. "Mommy—I mean, Amelia —" Her voice cut off, and she dropped her head in embarrassment.

Faith moved so that she could meet Mandi's eyes. "It's all good. I'm not a Little myself, but I've met Littles before. You're lucky to have a Mommy who looks after you so well."

The beaming smile Mandi sent her way almost blinded Faith. "She's the absolute best. Please do come and have dinner with us. It'd be awful if a disappointing time here ruined your day."

She acquiesced and went to change from the underwear she'd been wearing into something a little more appropriate for public spaces. When the three of them left the club together, Mandi took Amelia's hand and then, after checking with Faith, took her hand too.

Faith didn't know the last time someone had held her hand. It felt nice.

They made their way to a small diner, not too far from the club, and settled into a booth. The waitress was friendly when she took their orders and seemed vaguely bemused that all of them ended up ordering the same thing: burger and fries.

With anyone else, Faith would have imagined there might be some awkwardness, but Mandi was so engaging, she couldn't help but feel at home.

"You have to tell us all about you! What brought you to the club?"

"Well," said Faith. "I guess I wanted to meet new people and do some scenes. But I seem to kind of get it wrong with everyone."

"What do you mean?" asked Amelia, her tone kind, not accusatory.

"It seems like everyone knows what the unspoken rules are for a place like that. I've read all of the written rules, over and over, but nowhere does it say that being bluntly honest about what you want is a bad thing. And yet, every time I told people what it was I was looking for when they asked, they looked at me strangely, or accused me of trying to top from the bottom."

Mandi pulled a face. "Oh that sucks. People are so rubbish when it comes to rules. Half the time they don't even know that they have them, which is so silly when it comes to"—she dropped her voice to a whisper—"kink. You're neurodiverse then?"

Faith nodded. "AuDHD, so a delightful combination of hating routine and needing routine at the same time."

That made Mandi gurgle with laughter. "I've got autism." She turned her head and lifted her hair from her ear to show off pretty pink earplugs. "So, I do understand. Mommy?"

"Yes, babygirl?"

"Maybe Faith would like Rawhide?"

Faith wasn't entirely certain what rawhide was. Maybe it was a type of leather flogger? But from the looks Amelia and Mandi exchanged, they were probably talking about something else altogether. "What's rawhide?"

Amelia paused as the waitress brought over their food and waited until she had left. "It's not a thing, it's a place. Rawhide Ranch. It's the resort where Mandi and I live. It is… accepting."

"Accepting?" Accepting of what? Of their queer relationship? Of Mandi being a Little…?

"It's a place for kinksters," explained Mandi. "There's a university, and a school, and there's a program for Littles and a program for service subs, and it's really nice. Some people visit and some people stay."

"And you both live there?"

Mandi's smile went all soft and melty, which hit Faith right in the solar plexus. She'd never felt anything that made her look like that. "I came to Rawhide when I was… I was lost." She reached out and squeezed Amelia's hand. "I was just going to visit, but then I met Amelia, and got a job as a librarian, and now I live there fulltime. We both do."

"It's a space where you're safe to be whoever you need to be," said Amelia. "Littles can be Little 24/7, if that's what they need. But there's also a Dungeon, and we have people come and stay for a week. The rules are laid out very clearly, and no one is going to be angry with you for saying what you need."

"That sounds like heaven," said Faith wistfully.

"Come and stay!" said Mandi, impetuously. "I mean, there's a screening process, and you'd have to apply, but I think you'd like it. And even if you don't find someone to play with, you'd be able to make new friends and hang out with me, and it'd be lovely!"

"It might not suit you," said Amelia. "Because

nowhere suits everyone, but it is a safe space, and it'd likely feel more welcoming than that club. Attending on your own must have been so daunting."

"It wasn't the best afternoon," said Faith. "I've been with friends before, but no one ever wants to play with me, and I thought it would hurt less if there weren't friends to witness that." She grabbed a fry and ate it slowly. "It just hurt in a different way."

"Well," said Mandi, "how about coming to visit Rawhide because you want to develop more of a community? Then if you play with someone, it's a nice surprise, rather than attending with that being your sole intention."

Faith hadn't been on vacation for a while, and she had accrued quite a lot of leave, and if she were honest with herself, the idea of spending time on a ranch, visiting with these lovely two women who knew nothing about her, but had been so caring—well, it just sounded lovely. "Maybe for just a weekend," she said.

CHAPTER Two

Faith didn't know what was more panty-dropping —Bex's smile or her accent. She'd noticed the woman as soon as she'd walked into the restaurant with Mandi. It was her first day at Rawhide Ranch, and Mandi had wanted to introduce her to Tay, and get some food, so they'd come down to the restaurant early, only to find Tay talking to someone else.

Bex had long dark hair, pulled up into a tight ponytail, and her clothes showed off the kind of curves Faith longed to bury her face in. She was drop-dead gorgeous, clearly very confident, and now *she'd* pulled out a chair for *Faith*.

Faith had no idea what to make of that.

"Thank you," she whispered, and took the seat, avoiding Mandi's look.

"This is Faith," said Mandi, introducing her. "And I'm Mandi."

"Nice to meet you," said Bex. "Are you residents here?"

"I am," said Mandi. "Tay's my roommate. But Faith here is visiting."

Faith looked up and found intense dark eyes watching her. "Hi," she offered nervously. She didn't know what had come over her. Usually she was chatty as anything, talking away, but there was something about this woman that radiated calmness and security and it was making Faith oddly anxious.

Usually, calm people evoked the same emotion in Faith. But not this time. This time it put her on edge, as if Bex saw something in her that Faith… well, that Faith didn't know what someone like Bex could possibly see in *her*.

"Hi, Faith," said Bex. "I'm visiting too. Are you in the Guest Wing?"

"Yes, I'm on the third floor," she said.

"Nice to meet you," said Tay, interrupting for a moment, and Faith pulled her eyes away from Bex's stare. "Are you veggie?"

"What? Oh, no, I'm not."

"Excellent," said Tay. "I'll make you all the same pasta." And then they headed to the kitchen before anyone could say another word.

"I hope you like pasta," said Mandi. "And I do promise you Tay is an excellent chef."

"I'm sure they are," said Faith, and snuck a look back at Bex.

Bex was still looking at her.

"So, what do you do?" asked Mandi, seemingly oblivious to the tension between Faith and Bex. That broke the spell slightly, and Bex turned towards Mandi as she answered.

"I'm a management consultant," said Bex. "Newly over here; living in Billings at the moment."

"Oh wow. Faith lives in Billings, too, don't you, Faith?"

Faith nodded wordlessly as Bex turned her gaze in Faith's direction once more. She could feel a flush staining her cheeks and asked hurriedly, "How do you like Billings, Bex?"

"It seems lovely, although"—Bex leaned in conspiratorially—"I must admit I spend most of my time working, so I haven't gotten to explore too much."

"You should show Bex around when you guys go back," said Mandi, and Faith realized Mandi may not have been as oblivious to the tension as she'd originally thought. "Faith works in Clay Studio."

"You're an artist?" asked Bex. "That's pretty cool."

"I work on a lot of their outreach programs," Faith explained. "And lead some of the classes."

"You must be pretty good," said Bex, admiringly. "Do you throw—is that the word?—clay very often?"

Faith threw clay pretty much every single day—she'd been wondering how she'd cope for even just a weekend at Rawhide without being able to do so. "I have an Instagram with some of my pots, if you'd like to see?"

Bex shuffled her chair round the table so she could get a closer look. Bex's thigh grazed hers and Faith found she could barely focus on getting her Instagram page up on her phone. It was as if every inch of her had been electrocuted. Goosebumps, hairs on end, butterflies in her stomach, everything she'd always read about in romance novels.

Both Mandi and Bex made oooing noises over Faith's work, and that warmed her. Most of her friends from home weren't all that interested in what she made. And while her colleagues were interested, everyone was so busy at work, they often didn't have time to talk about what they were working on outside of the programs.

"I really love it," she said. "There's something about it just being you, the clay and the wheel which is really calming. There's nothing much else that quiets my brain. Well, aside from—" Her words cut off and she could feel the flush in her cheeks deepen.

Bex laughed then, a deep sound that had Faith's nipples tighten and her pussy clench. "I think most people feel that way about those kinds of asides." She wasn't laughing at Faith, Faith knew that, but there was an edge in her words that had Faith avoiding her gaze.

The pasta came then, and it smelled incredible. A tomato sauce with a deep, rich flavor was ladled atop ravioli that tasted wildly good. Tay popped their head round the door of the kitchen, and nodded when they noted everyone was eating away quite happily.

"So, what is everyone here looking for?" asked Bex as she ate a forkful of pasta.

There was a long pause, and Faith nodded towards Mandi, to let her answer first. It'd give Faith longer to come up with an answer that wouldn't scare Bex away.

"Well, I found what I was looking for," said Mandi. "I work in the Littles' Library, and then I found my Mommy Domme in the Head Librarian here. We don't live together just yet, but that's the plan eventually." She smiled. "I came here looking for my Little side; through one thing and another, I'd kind of lost her, and Rawhide helped me find her again."

"How about you?" Bex addressed the question directly to Faith. "Are you a Little as well?"

Faith blinked, and Bex's smile faltered.

"Crap, did I fuck up?" She stopped speaking, eyes wide. "Shit, I'm not supposed to curse, am I?"

Faith couldn't help it, she burst out laughing, and the panic in Bex's eyes subsided somewhat.

Mandi looked rather amused. "Littles aren't allowed to curse, but"—she lowered her voice conspiratorially—"I still do sometimes. Mommy calls me her sweary princess."

"It's been a struggle," admitted Bex. "Americans curse a hell of a lot less than Brits do, and I do have a tendency to swear more than most."

Faith laughed. "It's okay, we won't tell on you. And you didn't mess up; I guess I'm just not used to people asking me that in a non-kink setting."

"A *non-kink*—you did read all that info I gave you about Rawhide, didn't you?" joked Mandi.

"Yes, but this isn't a dungeon or a playroom, it's a restaurant," said Faith. "And to answer your question, Bex, no, I'm not a Little. Just a run of the mill sub."

Bex met her eyes with a quiet smile. "Just a run of the mill sub, eh? They're usually the most fun to play with."

That damn flush was back, painting her cheeks, and making her want to squirm under the heat of Bex's gaze. "Oh yeah?" Faith gathered up all of her courage and tried her best to sass Bex back. "Well, that's only if the Domme isn't so up themselves that…" Her voice trailed off. "I mean that's only if…"

That flush in her cheeks felt almost painful this time. This was not fun. She pulled a face and looked at Bex. "I'm not very good at being funny, I'm afraid. But if I were, I'd say something sassy now instead of getting all flustered."

Bex's lips twitched, and she nudged Faith with her hand. "You're all good, hun. I'm not particularly funny myself. And getting a sub all flustered for the *right* reasons is utterly delicious." She paused, and then blushed herself. "Just like you."

Chapter Three

Apparently Bex was busting out *all* the cheesy lines.

But Faith was delicious. Undeniably so.

There was something about her that made Bex want to gently tease the other woman, but seeing her flustered, or even on the edge of being upset? Absolutely not. That was unacceptable.

She hadn't expected, however, to meet someone she wanted to top within the first two hours of arriving though. And from the way Faith's cheeks flamed every time she complimented her, she thought the brunette might feel the same way.

Bex was trying to include Mandi in the conversation too, but she couldn't help but be transfixed by Faith.

"I'm popping to the bathroom," said Mandi. "Back in a minute."

And then they were alone together.

The restaurant was starting to fill up, chattering Littles amongst the people clearly taking their lunch break whilst working. Soon the checker-colored tablecloths were covered in menus, drinks, and plates.

And yet, somehow, it felt as if they were the only ones in the room together. Like there was a bubble around the two of them.

Bex had heard of this phenomenon before, of course, but she'd always dismissed it as the ramblings of lesbians in love. But now…

"Look, Faith," said Bex, taking a risk. "I don't know what you were planning on doing this evening, but I've booked in to go down to the Dungeon. I *was* going to check it out, see if there's anyone I click with, but I was wondering if you'd like to come with me."

"Oh," said Faith, smiling shyly.

Bex crossed her fingers, and then her legs and toes for good measure.

"I mean, that sounds like it could be nice. Mandi said the Littles don't really use the Dungeon—that's why her and Amelia were in Billings when we met—and going on my own is a bit scary."

"But you've been to a dungeon before?"

Faith rolled her eyes, and Bex tried not to laugh at the other woman's response. "*Yes,* I've been to a dungeon before. Well, to a kink club, but it's a similar vibe."

"It is definitely a similar vibe, though I imagine here it's quieter and less overwhelming than a busy club might be. And I like the fact they have private playrooms. I'm not saying we have to play together tonight—although," she couldn't help herself adding, as if she had absolutely no chill whatsoever, "I would certainly not be averse to that—but going with someone to these places can make it less daunting. Would you like to go with me?"

"Yes please," breathed Faith, so enchantingly that Bex had to fight the urge to kiss her then and there.

She didn't want to get ahead of herself, certainly not on the first night at Rawhide Ranch, but at the same time, Faith was so delicious that Bex couldn't help but wish the rest of the afternoon away so they could descend into the Dungeon together.

When Mandi came back from the bathroom, she looked between the two of them, a smile creeping across her face, but neither Bex nor Faith said anything, and so general conversation resumed.

Mandi worked in the Littles' Library, with her Mommy Domme, and had been living on the Ranch for a number of months now. "Tay's my roommate," she said. "Though not for all that much longer. Mommy Amelia and I have been talking about when I'll move into her place." She wriggled on the spot and her clear excitement was very endearing. "You'll have to come and visit again, Faith, once I'm all settled in."

"I'd love that," said Faith. "That's exciting! But how does Tay feel about it?"

"How does Tay feel about what?" asked the chef, sliding into a seat next to them.

"About me moving out," said Mandi.

Tay pulled a face, and then dramatically threw themself onto the table. "I shall pine away without you, my dear, for every moment we're apart is hell for me!"

Mandi and Faith giggled, and Tay flashed them a grin, to show that they were not quite as overcome as all that after all.

"Ahem." The door to the kitchen was ajar, and a woman in a chef's jacket stood there, arms folded. Her hair was pulled back in a tight bun, and she looked far from impressed.

"Whoops!" said Tay, and picked themself up quickly. "Duty calls." Bounding over to the chef, they shot the older woman an irrepressible grin. "Chef Guilia."

"Tay." Chef Guilia looked unimpressed. "Not during service."

"Yes, chef," they answered, shooting a mock-worried face over their shoulder and then hurrying back into the kitchen.

After that interlude, lunch came to an end. Bex said goodbye to Mandi and Faith, lifting Faith's hand to kiss it in what must have been the cringiest move she'd ever made. It was worth it to see Faith dissolve into giggles.

She headed back upstairs to her suite, sat on the couch and decided to call Riley.

The call was answered rather quickly, and her best friend's face filled the screen. "Well, hello there, Bexy. Found yourself a cowgirl yet?"

Bex pulled a face at her friend. "I'm sorry, who amongst us is dating a MILF?"

Wendy's head popped into frame. "Hi, Bex."

"Oh shit, sorry, Wendy. I was only teasing Riley."

Wendy smiled. "She probably deserved it." They kissed and she stood up. "I'll see you a bit later, Mistress."

"Absolutely," said Riley, with the sappiest look on her face. It would have been sickening if it hadn't been so sweet. "So. Back to cowgirls."

"There aren't any cowgirls as such…"

"There's a but there," said Riley, her voice colored with enthusiasm. "Please tell me you've found *someone.* We both know you don't do well without a regular release."

Bex rolled her eyes and leaned back against the arm of the couch. "That's what vibrators are for, Riley. I've been getting myself off very satisfactorily every night."

"For *six months*," pointed out Riley. And it wasn't like she was wrong. Vibrators took the edge off, but they never quite got Bex *there* the way a woman's touch could. "Anyway, stop avoiding the question. Who is she?"

"Faith," said Bex. "Her name is Faith and she's sweet and kind of quiet, and we're going to check out the Dungeon together tonight."

"Sounds promising," said Riley, waggling her eyebrows.

There was an uncomfortable feeling somewhere in Bex's stomach, like she didn't approve of Riley being suggestive about Faith—even though the fact that they were going to the Dungeon together later spoke volumes.

Riley read Bex's change in body language—even over video—and her face went serious. "Shit, you actually like her. Like *like her* like her."

Bex tried to protest, but Riley was having none of it.

"You can't fall in love out there," she said. "You'll never come home!"

Sighing, Bex closed her eyes. "It's not home for me Riley, not anymore." It had been a long time since Bex had felt at home somewhere. She felt safe with Riley, had friends back in the UK, but nowhere had quite felt right. And after her dad had died, Bex had gotten a transfer out of the country sharpish. That way she didn't have to deal with relatives who all of a sudden gave a shit about her dad.

She'd been the one to look after him through those last years, balancing a demanding career with his care, and once he'd died, she hadn't wanted to be near anything or anyone that reminded her of him.

"I'm sorry, Bex," said Riley. "I don't know, I just thought one day you'd settle back down over here."

"I'm not ruling anything out," Bex said, "but I'm also not deciding on any of that right now. I have a good job, and damn it, Riley, I'm on holiday! I don't want to have to talk about this shit."

"No," said Riley. "You want to talk about *Faith*."

Bex pulled a face.

"Fine, fine, I'll stop teasing. What're you wearing to the Dungeon tonight then? If you like this girl that much, you're going to want to make an impression. Come on, what did you pack?"

It was a little like being back at university again,

picking out clothes for a night out, only Riley had seen all of Bex's kinkiest outfits.

"You don't want to come on too strong," she pointed out. "If Faith's as quiet as you say she is, you don't want to scare her off by going full-leather catsuit."

Bex shot her a look. "When have I ever worn a catsuit? Where would I even get one that fit me?"

"There are plus-size designers," protested Riley, but she knew Bex was right. "Come on then, what were you thinking?"

"Sheer black tights with the seam up the back, black lacy bra, black blazer."

Riley nodded approvingly. "Showing off all your best assets—legs, tits and curves. And your hair?"

"Down." Bex fingered her ponytail. "I think Faith would like it if my hair was down."

She wondered what else Faith liked, and hoped beyond all hope that she was going to get to find out for herself.

CHAPTER Four

Waiting by the elevator, Faith couldn't stop bouncing on the spot. Mandi had helped her get ready, once she'd finished her shift in the Littles' Library, and the two of them had gotten all excited. She'd eaten a decent dinner and had plenty of water.

Her pulse raced, and she couldn't help but stim, fingers fluttering by her sides. She'd dressed up, as best she could: a cute black dress, with a short skirt that flirted around her knees; a bra that did what it could with what little she had; and comfortable ballet flats, because even though heels made her legs look great, Faith hated how they made her feet feel.

Mandi had declared her perfection, and Amelia had said she looked "very nice" when she'd come to pick up Mandi for their date night.

Even so, Faith had shuffled about her suite until five minutes before the time they'd agreed to meet.

The Dungeon opened at 9 p.m., and Bex had promised to get the elevator up to Faith's floor, so she wouldn't have to go down on her own. She was grateful for that.

She still couldn't quite believe Bex wanted to go with her. For all Mandi's gushing over her outfit, Faith knew she wasn't really anything special to look at. That wasn't her being down on herself, it was just an objective fact. Faith had seen what pretty and beautiful women looked like, and she knew she didn't really fit any of those molds. She was tall and slender; she was all soft and curvy. She was a mid-ground. A standard person. And Bex seemed like she was used to anything but standard.

Elevator doors dinged and opened.

Bex stepped out.

Yeah, Bex was certainly not standard.

Long, shapely legs, with thighs that dimpled beneath sheer material, made their way up to where Bex's black blazer dipped in, flaring out over wide hips and a rounded stomach.

And her breasts.

Faith had to fight to stop staring her breasts, encased in black lace and threatening to spill over the top of the material.

"Hey," said Bex.

"Murgh," said Faith. She actually said "Murgh," as if her entire brain had short circuited the moment she'd seen Bex.

"Gods, you look great," said Bex, and she held out her hand for Faith to twirl on the spot for her.

She twirled, and her skirt rose up and spun round her, hinting at the lingerie beneath.

Bex made a strangled sound, and Faith was pleased to note she might not be the only one poleaxed in this moment.

"You okay?" she asked sweetly, and Bex laughed.

"Fuck, no. How the hell am I supposed to be all cool and calm and collected, when you're out here looking like that?"

Well, wasn't that the sweetest reaction?

"Shall we…?" She nodded towards the open elevator door.

"Oh Gods, yes, yes. Please, after you."

They stood together as the doors closed, side by side, and neither of them said a word. Faith snuck a glance at

Bex, who was clearly doing the same thing at the exact same moment. There was a pause and then they both burst out laughing.

"I'm a bit nervous," said Faith. "I have been to sex clubs before—I wasn't lying about that—but I've never really played in public. People usually find me a tad too..." Her voice trailed off. She didn't want to put Bex off, but at the same time it would be better to be upfront now. At least that way she wouldn't build her hopes up all evening only to have them dashed. "I've got AuDHD, so when people ask me what I want, I've answered them. Only it doesn't seem like they actually want to know, because when I do, they accuse me of topping from the bottom." She took a deep breath. "It's all very confusing really, and I'm not exactly sure what people want from a sub. There doesn't seem to be a set of rules I can follow."

The elevator dinged as it came to rest on the lower level, and the doors opened.

Faith didn't move forward. She raised her head, meeting Bex's eyes head on, almost defiantly. Fuck it. If she was going to do this, she was going to do this.

Bex put a hand out to hold the door, but waved back the large, tattooed man who came to greet them. "One sec please."

"Sure." He took a few steps back, out of earshot, but keeping them in his eyeline.

"Look, I don't know who you've met before, but they sound like arseholes. Part of negotiation is talking about what you want, what you like. That's not topping from the bottom—and frankly, I've never even really understood that phrase anyway. If you want high protocol, go somewhere like the Training House. Otherwise, a sub is not a slave unless otherwise negotiated." She shook her head in frustration, and her long hair moved about her.

"So, if we decide we want to talk about… *playing*, well then, I will want to know all the things you want. But until then, try not to stress too much, pickle."

"Pickle?" Faith asked.

Bex brushed a hand over her face in embarrassment. "It's a term of endearment, I promise. Now, do you actually want to go to the Dungeon, or would you rather hit the cinema they've got upstairs? I'm easy either way."

Faith realized she believed Bex. That if she changed her mind and wanted to go somewhere else, Bex would happily go along with whatever she decided. "Dungeon," she said firmly, and stepped out and smiled up at the very large, tattooed security guard. "We're here to visit the Dungeon." Her voice was clear, and he smiled at her.

"Absolutely, miss. It's just reopened now, so I think you two are the first ones in."

Faith tried not to wriggle with excitement, as they stood before the double doors. When they swung open, a large open space was revealed. Across from them there was an area where visitors could look down into the play space where purple and amber lighting drew the onlooker's attention to various areas including ones where Faith could see a spanking bench and a St. Andrew's Cross.

Bex headed over to the bar, and Faith turned to join her, smiling shyly when the other woman asked what she wanted to drink. "Just a coke for me please," she said. "I don't drink if there's a chance I might be playing."

"Good girl," said Bex, and she hadn't said it *like that*, but Faith felt it deep in her core anyway. She fought for a few moments, before giving in and letting her smile blossom into a grin. Her fingers stimmed again, marking out patterns on the wood of the bar, and though Bex looked down and noticed, she didn't tell Faith to stop. "You okay there, pickle? Not too nervous?"

She shook her head. "I don't think so."

"Good. Why don't we take our drinks and go and sit in the lounge area, over there. That way we can have a bit of chat before lots of people arrive and it gets a bit noisier."

CHAPTER *Five*

Bex was suffering from the most acute case of gay panic she'd ever experienced.

If she'd thought that Faith was delicious before, in this outfit she was delectable. Bex was having to concentrate doubly hard to make sure her sentences made sense, because all she wanted to do was to spread Faith's legs and eat her out until she gave up all her secrets.

As if voicing her desires was Faith topping from the bottom. She'd never heard anything so ridiculous in all her life. There wasn't anything the remotest bit Domme-y about Faith.

She was fairly certain she was stubborn—there was a streak of determination in her Bex wanted to see more of —but she didn't want to take charge of the evening. Faith was happy to let Bex lead on that.

And Bex wanted to.

They sat on the couch, and Faith jumped onto it, sitting in a way that only someone with ADHD would, and Bex swore that her skirt bounced up enough for a hint of black lace to show.

If Bex was looking.

Which she had determined not to do.

"So what do you like?" asked Faith.

"I like whatever my girl likes," said Bex, "and I'm not just saying that. Nothing gets me off harder than seeing a sub enjoy themselves so completely. So, you're just going to have to tell me all your deepest desires." Her voice had deepened slightly, and she didn't know if Faith could hear the strain in it, the desperation.

Bex didn't know when she'd turned into a horny teenager, but it was round about from the first moment she'd laid eyes on Faith. So well put together and presentable. Bex just wanted to ruin her. Muss her all up, and have Faith gasping her pleasure out, over and over.

"Oh," breathed Faith.

"But I need some of that directness you've mentioned. If," she added in a bit of a panic, "you're interested in playing with me. I'm sorry, Faith, pickle, I've come on a bit hard, haven't I?"

"It's quite alright," said Faith, reaching out to pat Bex's hand. "I really am quite interested in playing with you, too. Only, maybe not out here." Faith looked out across the room, and something shuttered in her eyes. "I'm not sure I want people to watch me."

"There are private playrooms," said Bex, and then added curiously. "Do you mind me asking why not? I'm not trying to change your mind; I just want to know. I want to understand."

There was a slight pause before Faith nodded. "I don't want people to laugh at me."

"Laugh at—why on earth would people laugh at you?"

"If I get it wrong. I don't want to get it wrong, but if I do, I'd rather there not be a whole audience for my humiliation."

Bex was vaguely aware of her hands clenching tight. She loosened them and smoothed down her blazer, trying to gather her thoughts. The last thing she wanted Faith to feel was scared or nervous, and if public play set her off this badly, then it was out of the question.

It made her wonder—made her worry—about the experiences Faith might have had in the past.

"The only way to mess up in my book, is to not use a safe word when you need to. That puts you in danger, and that's the only thing I'd get cross or stressed about."

"What safe word should I use?"

Bex chuckled. "That's up to you, pickle. It's not my place to tell you what word you should be using."

Faith had a think for a moment, and then said firmly, "Watermelon."

"Watermelon?"

"Watermelon. It's my favorite fruit, so I'm unlikely to forget it, but it's also something that we'd be unlikely to reference in a scene. And it's red, so it works as a traffic light. Then banana for yellow, and apple for green."

"You want to use fruits as traffic lights?"

"I like fruit," Faith said. "And besides, it means when I next eat fruit, I'll think of this night." And Bex was charmed all over again.

"Do you know what you'd like to do?"

Faith started to get flustered, and Bex reached out to hold her hands. Somehow, it seemed to calm the other woman, and Faith took a deep breath and nodded. "Maybe if we focus on one or two things? And see if we can get one of the private playrooms?"

"Of course." Bex waited. She wasn't sure what Faith was going to suggest, and her mind spun at all the possibilities laid out before the two of them.

"Maybe we could see if there's a St. Andrew's Cross in one of the private rooms? And do some impact play?"

"We can do that," said Bex, smiling. "Would you like the play to remain strictly non-sexual?"

The look Faith shot her was all wide-eyes and innocent longing. Fuck. "Would you like to—"

"How about—" interjected Bex before Faith could

start centering Bex again, "you just share with me what *you* want."

Wide eyes blinked rapidly. "But—"

Bex didn't even say anything this time; merely raised an eyebrow and waited.

"Fine. No, I would like it if our play was sexual as well."

"Me too." The frisson of excitement that ran through Bex was hard to hide. "Shall we do opt in?"

Faith nodded. "I'd like kisses, please. And I'd like to keep my dress on, but I'm happy with hands and fingers beneath it."

"Over lingerie or…" Bex let her voice trail off suggestively.

Faith flushed. "Under is fine. I just don't want to get fully naked here, in case someone walks in that I don't know and…"

"I get it," said Bex, and squeezed her hand reassuringly. "All of those things sound good to me. I suppose I was wondering how you'd feel about me using my mouth on you."

The noise Faith made was unintelligible.

"Is that a yes?"

She nodded very quickly. "Yes, that's a yes."

"Okay, so we've got clothes on, though touching beneath fabric is all good. Yes to kisses, yes to fingers and hands, and yes to my mouth. Would you like me to fingerfuck you?" Her words were deliberately blunt. Bex had never liked euphemisms.

"Yes." Her directness was rewarded with a connected look and a slight smile. Faith's chest was flushing now, as well as her face; the small swell of her breasts turning pink. "And would you like me to touch you?"

"I think I'd prefer that in a bed, besides, you're going

to be strung up on a St. Andrew's Cross for me. I'm not sure you'll have free hands. But kisses I'll take aplenty, if you're offering?"

Tentatively, Faith inched closer to Bex on the sofa. "I'm offering," she said.

CHAPTER *Six*

No one had ever looked at Faith like Bex did. It was electrifying.

The brunette licked her lips, and Faith followed the flick of Bex's tongue, trying not to imagine how it would feel against her clit, against her nipples.

"You're staring at my lips, Faith," said Bex, her voice a rumble of desire.

"That's because I'm waiting for you to kiss me." Faith had thought that she'd made her intentions very clear, but apparently Bex needed some guidance. "If you'd like, I'm happy to take the lead?"

"Oh no you don't, you cheeky thing you," said Bex, and she pulled Faith to her in a way that had Faith all melty in her arms.

Bex's head bent and, closing her eyes, Faith gave herself over to the kiss. It was gentle, not too overwhelming, but there was an intensity to it that had her wriggle in place and sigh her pleasure into Bex's mouth.

She ran her hand up and caught her fingers in Bex's long hair she'd left down for the evening. The strands felt like silk against her skin.

When Bex pulled back, the two of them paused for a moment, breathing decidedly more heavily than they had a few moments earlier.

"Good kiss?" Faith asked, just checking.

"Fucking great kiss," said Bex, and leaned forward to kiss Faith again.

Faith decided that she was quite alright doing nothing but kissing Bex for the rest of her life. Teeth nipped at her lower lip, and then Bex alternated between

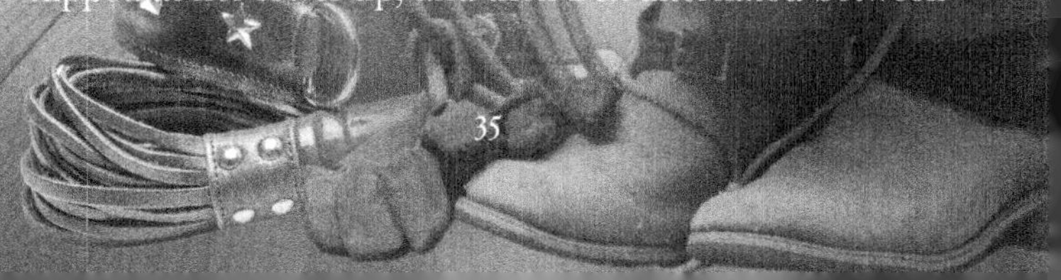

nibbling and sucking on it. It felt like a hickey for the mouth and Faith had never experienced anything like it.

"More of that," she said, pressing her fingers to where her lip throbbed. "That was awesome, I want more of that."

"Your wish is my command," said Bex, and then rolled her eyes at the words. "I seriously don't know what you do to me, Faith. I promise I'm not usually this cheesy."

Faith didn't mind it though. It was kind of nice to have someone go all gooey and soft over her kisses. She liked that. "Should we have a look at the private playrooms?" she asked.

"Good call. Come on you." Bex jumped up and held out a hand to Faith.

She took it, liking the firmness of Bex's grip, and followed as Bex headed over to a man wearing black slacks and a black shirt. There was a gold band around his biceps. According to the information Bex had read about the Dungeon, the uniform identified the man as a Dungeon Monitor.

"Hey, how do we book one of the private playrooms?"

"Usually people book in advance, but I can have a look through the set ups and see if there are any free for you?" offered the DM.

"Yes please," they said simultaneously.

"One with a St. Andrew's Cross," added Faith breathlessly. "If possible."

He met her eyes and smiled at her enthusiasm. "I'm sure we can manage something." He typed a couple of things out on a tablet, scanned through and nodded. "Yup, room four is available. You should both be okay, height-wise, but if you need any extenders, there should be some in the armoire. There are various implements in there as well. Simply return whatever you use in the basket beside the cabinet unless you want to add it to your personal collection. In that case, inform a service submissive. They will clean the implement and return it to your suite." He pointed to where a young man dressed in black pants and a lilac shirt was stacking some folded towels into one of the many armoires spread throughout the Dungeon.

"Great, thank you," said Bex, and she caught hold of Faith's hand and ushered her ahead, down the corridor to the playrooms.

The lighting was purple and amber here too, but when they entered room four, Faith noticed a remote with instructions for changing the lighting.

"Can we have low-level standard lighting?" she asked. "No one really looks great in amber, and for sensory reasons, I don't really like having the lights turned all the way up."

"Go ahead, pickle, and adjust the lighting to how you'd like it." Bex was over by the St. Andrew's Cross, fiddling with the attached cuffs. "I love the fact that this is a smaller cross. It's not going to be too tall for you at all!"

As Faith watched, Bex undid her blazer and tossed it onto the couch in the corner. "What're your aftercare needs?"

"Huh?" Faith couldn't think about anything other than having that lusciously curvy body pressed up against hers. The spread of Bex's hips, the swell of her stomach, the size of her thighs… everything about her was utterly transfixing.

"Aftercare, pickle, what aftercare needs do you have?"

"Oh," Faith blinked furiously in an attempt to refocus her mind away from "holy crap Bex is gorgeous" thoughts. "Ummm... water? And cuddles. Maybe blankets too?"

Bex nodded towards the couch, which was covered in blankets, and had a couple of unopened bottles of water on the floor. "Damn, this place really is good! Now, to the armoire!"

The armoire was made of a dark cherry wood, that seemed to shine as they approached it. "Usually, I'd use my own flogger," said Bex, "but I didn't like to assume we'd be playing together this evening. Let's have a look at what they have to offer."

When opened, the range of toys made Faith's eyes widen, and even Bex gave a low whistle.

"We don't have to use *all* of them, do we?" asked Faith, eyeing a particularly vicious looking cane nervously.

"Not at all, pickle," said Bex as she moved to stand behind Faith and wrapped her arms around her.

The little breath Faith let out was one of relief. There was something in her that said *finally* when she was in Bex's arms. Something that felt right.

Bex froze up in that way Faith was coming to recognize as slight panic, and she wriggled backward until they fit together perfectly and said, "No need to panic. This is lovely."

"It is," said Bex. "It really is."

Neither of them spoke for a few moments. They just stood there, Bex's arms enveloping Faith in her Bex-ness, breathing steadily.

"There are so many things this evening could be," said Bex, eventually. *She* sounded nervous now, and Faith was relieved to realize it wasn't just her. "The potential is almost terrifying, because whatever it is, I don't want to fuck it up. I don't want to fuck *this* up."

Faith twisted around in Bex's arms and then leaned in and kissed her hard. "This evening will be what we make of it. I trust you. We've got this."

CHAPTER Seven

The enormity of Faith's trust felt like a huge weight. Topping someone wasn't a responsibility Bex ever took lightly, but somehow this scene felt more delicate, more fragile than any she'd taken part in before.

It was, she thought, because she cared so much. She hadn't even known Faith for twenty-four hours, and yet everything in Bex's body was yelling at her that she was home.

If she hadn't done as much therapy as she had, it would probably have been wildly triggering.

Home wasn't something Bex really considered much, on a day-to-day basis. If anything, she usually tried to avoid thinking about it, because home was mushy peas and fish and chips on a Friday night, plonked on the sofa in her dad's house, watching crappy panel shows and swearing at the tv. It was union rallies with her dad shouting for workers' rights and teasing her about her job as a management consultant. It was every football match she'd ever gone to, singing rowdy songs on the terraces with her dad.

Home was her dad.

And her dad was dead.

It shouldn't be possible for a woman she barely knew to bring all of those memories, all of those feelings associated with home flooding back, and yet somehow Faith had done just that.

"Bex?" Faith asked. "Are you okay?"

She met dark eyes and smiled. "You feel… familiar," she said, not wanting to say Faith felt like home, because

Bex knew that was wild talk. "I don't know how, or why, but it feels as if—"

"As if I've known you all my life," finished Faith. "Yes, I feel that too."

"It just took me by surprise for a moment," said Bex. "That's all."

Faith planted one of those hard, short kisses on her again, and Bex couldn't help but grin. The world's problems could probably be sorted with one of those intense Faith kisses, she thought.

"Come on, pickle, let's pick out some implements to play with."

They'd looked through the armoire together, marveling at the wide range that Rawhide had on offer and settled on a handful of different floggers.

Bex tested each one, doing a figure-of-eight in front of her, and then testing each one on her arm. She wanted to know how they felt for herself before she used them on Faith. Whether they were thuddy or had a sharp sting, were they soft or rough. They'd picked out an assortment of floggers, which meant a variety of sensations and Bex wanted to make sure that one led into the next seamlessly.

And then it was time.

She took Faith's hand and led her over to the cross. "I'm going to attach you facing the cross first," she said. "But just for now. After I've had my fill of flogs, I'm going to lie you down on that couch and eat you out until you scream."

"Sounds like a plan," said Faith, as if they were planning a day to the beach or something. She really was too adorable.

Bex started from the top. She stretched each of Faith's arms up until she could encircle Faith's wrists with the cuffs. They were faux-leather, probably a type of pleather, with soft cushioning on the inside. Vital if Faith was going to have them round her wrists for any extended period of time. Tightening them up, she adjusted the height so that Faith's arms lifted higher above her head, and Faith tugged on them experimentally. "Just wanted to make sure I couldn't get out," she said to Bex, grinning.

"There's something sassy about you, isn't there?" said Bex. She wasn't complaining. She thought Faith was so darn cute when she answered back and tested Bex's boundaries as a Domme.

"Yes, Bex," said Faith, her accent suddenly very pronounced.

"Well, that had a cowgirl's twang to it," muttered Bex under their breath. "Riley would love that."

"Who's Riley?" demanded Faith, catching the words.

"My best friend," said Bex. "And no, I've never slept with her. Never particularly wanted to either, but any case, she'd love that accent of yours."

"How'd you like it?" asked Faith slyly.

"Oh, I like it just fine," said Bex. "It's very cute indeed." She ran her hand down Faith's back, stroking her through the fabric, and watched as Faith's concentration shifted. "Shall we talk about your accent some more?"

"No, thank you, Bex," said Faith dreamily. "Floggings please."

There was a moment when Bex considered teasing her about that, about being demanding, but she stopped just in time. Faith wasn't being demanding or playing up. She was just expressing what she wanted, clearly.

That deserved a reward.

Bex prepped the first flogger, and swung, the sound a sharp *crack.*

Faith gasped, and then sagged against her restraints.

"What are those legs doing together?" asked Bex, using her foot to nudge them apart. That had Faith shifting on the spot. Changing a sub's center of gravity—particularly when tied with their hands above their head—really made a difference to how they stood. "A bit more, *that's* it. Good girl, Faith."

Even though Faith was facing away from her, Bex could sense the smile that spread across the other woman's face.

"Would you like more, Faith?"

"I wasn't even really aware that you'd started."

That was sass Bex hadn't expected, and she dealt with it more from instinct than anything else and delivered an almighty wallop.

A strike like that had made more experienced subs than Faith cry, but Faith didn't cry. She threw her head back and *laughed.* The joy pealed through the playroom, and Bex was taken aback but just how happy Faith was. She'd played with people who enjoyed impact play, of course, but not with such deep-throated pleasure.

"Come on, Bex, give it to me!"

Faith was being demanding now, but it didn't bother Bex, didn't make her feel like she was failing as a Domme. If anything, it made her appreciate Faith's complete trust in her. She'd been hurt before, and she wasn't holding anything back because of it. Instead she was full-throated in her approval of Bex's technique.

As stroke after stroke fell, Faith remained open, happy and exuberant.

CHAPTER Eight

Faith was floating.

Subspace was her happy place, the space where nothing and no one mattered anymore. It was like walking into a white room, closing the door behind you, and putting your feet up. Nothing to distract, nothing to take away your attention.

Nothing but sensations.

Faith didn't know why she loved some sensations, and others she couldn't stand. There was something in her brain chemistry that meant extra loud noises, and very bright lights, and the touch of certain things made her skin crawl. She had earplugs and sunglasses, but most of the time she just avoided being in situations where she knew she'd be set off.

Or at least have somewhere to go afterward, to recharge.

But for some reason, the sensations of impact play didn't set her off. Perhaps it was due to the fact she found them physically grounding, that they kept her in her body, present, when her mind wanted to go off wandering.

Either way, it was fucking great.

And it was even better when Bex was the one delivering the sensations.

Bex knew not to make every stroke the same, knew to vary the placement and weight each time. But the rhythm... The rhythm kept on and it was that which lulled Faith deeper and deeper into subspace.

After her first mouthing off, they'd fallen into an easy pattern, punctuated with Faith's laughter. She didn't know when she'd ever laughed so much.

But slowly, surely, her laughter died away and Faith found herself floating more and more.

Her wrists hung a little more from the cuffs, and she found herself slumped against the cross.

"Hey." Bex's voice was up against her ear. Intimate. "Hey there, pickle. How are you doing? Where are you at?"

"Apples," she whispered. "Apples and pears and kiwis and"—she was babbling now—"cucumbers, though are cucumbers a fruit? Do you think cucumbers are a fruit, Bex?"

Bex chuckled. "I think someone's had enough."

"*Nooooooooo*," Faith wailed. "I want *more*! More flogs, *pleeeeeeease*."

More chuckles. "I think perhaps we take a break, let you rehydrate. If you want to go for round two after that, then we surely can, pickle."

She loosened the cuffs from Faith's wrists, and Faith almost fell into Bex's arms, and only just managed to pull herself back upright.

"Oh you sweetheart! Come on, come sit over here."

Still giggling, Faith followed Bex over to the couch and threw herself down onto it dramatically. Her legs flung upward and back down, and Bex moved forward quickly to make sure Faith didn't accidentally kick her ankles on something hard.

She moved up onto the couch next to Faith, and positioned herself so that Faith could rest her head on Bex's lap.

"Hey, pickle, you still feeling all floaty?"

"*Sooooooo* floaty." Faith giggled again. "Floaty… it's a funny word. Why didn't you let me apple, Bex?"

"Because," said Bex, "you'd clearly had enough. I'm not an arsehole; when a sub needs a break, I give them a break. And you—my little pickle—needed a break."

"I'm *fine*," said Faith, but she was aware she was waving her arms around a little too aggressively. Why was she doing that? She blinked; it felt like the blink was taking forever. "Bex, I feel drunk."

"I know, sweetheart," said Bex. And then there was a bottle of water against her lips, and Bex told her to open up and drink for her.

Faith did, and it was refreshing and gorgeous and holy crap, just how deep into subspace had she slipped?

With the water came the sudden realization of how bizarre she was acting, and Faith sat bolt upright, ready to apologize.

But Bex just pulled her back down to her lap. "You're all good, pickle. You're just going to rest a little bit and make it back up from subspace before we do anything else. There's no rush. I've booked the room for the whole night. We can sleep here if we want to."

Faith shot Bex a look.

"Or not!" Bex said laughing. "Not a fan of camping then?"

"Absolutely not," said Faith. "I'm a woman of a certain age. I need a proper bed, thank you very much."

"A woman of a… aren't you in your twenties?"

"Yes." Faith wasn't entirely certain what that had to do with anything. "And I have become accustomed to a certain way of life. Namely sleeping in a proper bed with a proper mattress."

Bex sounded more than slightly bemused. "I shall escort you back to your room once we are done then, and you can get back into your bed."

That sounded right, only there was something about it that Faith wasn't entirely convinced by. "*We* can get into my bed. It's big enough for the both of us. And besides, we can't have you roaming the halls on your own, Bex. Anything could happen!"

Bex nodded and stroked her hair. "Whatever you want, pickle."

Slowly, subspace retreated and Faith found her thoughts becoming less jumbled and more coherent. She didn't say anything at first, just continued to lie with her head in Bex's lap, letting the Domme stroke her hair. This was very peaceful. Even with subspace receding further and further backward, Faith found herself smiling.

"I went pretty deep, huh?" she asked.

"Just a little bit," said Bex. "I guess I should take it as a compliment, though I wonder if I should have stopped earlier."

"I'm glad you didn't," said Faith. "I really was having the best time. But I wasn't joking about my bed. It's going to get busy in the Dungeon I think; would you like to come back? And we can continue what we started..."

CHAPTER Nine

Leaving the Dungeon had felt a little awkward. Bex had managed to rescue her blazer from where she'd tossed it across the sofa, and Faith had straightened her dress, and tried to tidy her hair so it didn't give off "just been fucked vibes" quite so much.

The two of them had smiled shyly at the tattooed security guard as they'd walked by, and he'd smiled back at them, nodding at them over the top of his book—which appeared to be a romance novel.

They held hands in the elevator way up to the third floor, and Bex started planning all the ways in which she was going to make this delightful for Faith. But she needn't have bothered because the moment they entered Faith's suite, she backed Bex up against the wall and kissed her.

Turned out that Bex *loved it* when Faith backed her up against the wall and kissed her.

It did all kinds of funny things to her knees.

Faith's enthusiasm, and the little desperate whimpers she emitted as they kissed, were overwhelmingly adorable. So much so that Bex's knees threatened to give way altogether.

It wasn't that she was trying to take charge though—if you didn't understand who Faith was, what she wanted, Bex supposed it could have been interpreted as topping from the bottom, but she understood that wasn't what this was.

This was pure, unadulterated joy.

Bex was reminded of those peals of laughter whilst she'd flogged Faith earlier.

Sex had always been fun—kink even more so—but she'd never experienced it as joyous before.

Faith broke away and laughed. "Come on, my bed's this way."

It was Bex's turn to back Faith up, but this time it wasn't against a wall, she kept guiding Faith backward until the mattress of the bed met the back of Faith's knees.

"Oops," laughed Faith, and Bex slipped her hand into Faith's hair and pulled the other woman flush against her.

"Are you ready?"

Trusting eyes blinked up at her. "Absolutely. Are *you* ready?"

Was she? Bex wasn't entirely certain sleeping with Faith wouldn't completely upend her life, but there was an insistent tugging in her heart that told her this was happening, so she was going to have to get used to it, and sharpish.

"Strip for me," Bex said, and stepped back to watch Faith shed her clothes, as she started on the buttons of her own blazer.

Faith couldn't meet her eyes as she shyly slipped the dress from her shoulders, and stepped out of it, leaving her clad only in black-lace knickers and a matching bra, and those adorable ballet flats. And then she toed her shoes off and in doing so, she took Bex's breath away.

"You are so fucking gorgeous," Bex told her. "So delicious. I can't wait to eat you all up."

Faith's gaze flew upward and caught on Bex's bra.

The light in the suite was better than in the Dungeon, and as Faith was no longer tied up to a St. Andrew's Cross, she could take in all of Bex. And there was a *lot* of Bex to take in. She wasn't usually self-conscious about her full-figure—she'd had enough women begging to sub for her at Riley's club to have zero doubts about her hotness—but somehow, she felt vulnerable in this moment.

Faith must have sensed something because she moved close and slipped her arm around Bex's waist. "I wish you could see yourself the way I do." She stepped back and deliberately looked over Bex.

Bex found herself ducking her head, barely breathing as if awaiting Faith's approval.

When the other woman stepped back, her finger under Bex's chin coaxed her gaze upward until she could see Faith's smile. "I cannot wait for you to ravish me."

She wasn't sure what to say, how to even *speak* after those words.

Faith slipped her underwear down and off, sat on the bed, took off her bra and leaned back and looked at Bex. "Your turn to strip for me."

Bex didn't sub.

She didn't switch.

She just didn't.

But for Faith she found herself reaching behind and taking off her bra, and Faith's sharp gasp on an inbreath was a wonderful reward. "Like what you see?" Her shy grin at the other woman added levity to the moment, and she felt a bit more comfortable. This wasn't about Faith topping her—it was about the two of them being vulnerable *with each other*.

"Fuck yes," said Faith, slipping to her knees at the foot of the bed and reaching up to roll down Bex's tights. Her hands were cool and dry, not as soft as the rest of her, but as they grazed her skin, Bex couldn't help but gasp.

"I want to taste you."

She looked down and Faith was staring up at her, smiling softly.

"I thought I'm the one in charge here," Bex said, but she was laughing.

"You are," said Faith. "And I would like the opportunity to worship you."

Bex took Faith's hands and pulled her up to standing. "How about this—I lay you back and feast my fill, and then after, I sit on your face and ride your tongue?"

The delight in Faith's face was utterly endearing. "I think I'd be okay with that."

"Good," said Bex.

Faith bounced backward on the bed, and then scooted up the mattress in the most endearing wriggly manner. "Come on then." She spread her legs. "Come feast."

CHAPTER Ten

Faith thought she'd never forget the look on Bex's face as she spread her legs before her. Hungry and desperate and yearning all at once. She reached out her hand, and Bex took it, moving up to kiss Faith's lips hard, and then moving down to kiss her other lips.

Fingers stroked through her curls, and Bex's thumb reached up to brush against Faith's clit. She gasped. The touch was intoxicating, and then Bex replaced her thumb with her tongue and Faith's back arched all the way off the bed and she made a noise she'd never heard herself make before—something halfway between a squeak and hum. It was bizarre.

She felt Bex pause, tongue withdrawing slightly, and then as the mattress moved, she realized the other woman was laughing.

Looking down the bed, she mock-glared at the brunette. "I don't know what you think's so funny!"

Bex couldn't speak, laughing so hard she was wheezing.

"It's not *that* funny," said Faith.

Bex bent her head and licked Faith's clit again.

And Faith made the noise again. Gods that was embarrassing, and—okay—a tiny bit funny too.

She giggled, and this time, Bex's tongue circled her clit before her lips drew it into her mouth. The intensity of the suction had Faith's eyes rolling up into the back of her head, and she fell back against the pillows, no longer caring if Bex was laughing or not, because if she kept that up . . .

Faith swore, and Bex chuckled. "You're cute when you come apart," she said.

Faith considered answering her back, giving Bex some sass, but soon all thoughts were swept away by the sensations that flooded her body.

Sexual touch felt different from impact play.

Impact play was all about becoming so overwhelmed her mind stopped trying to process each and every little thing that was happening to her, and she just gave herself over to the sensations.

But sexual touch was different for Faith. It made her feel vulnerable, peeling back layers to reveal the soft sensitive center within. To reveal her.

And even though the acuteness of these sensations felt overwhelming, they also felt incredibly intimate.

The two of them felt intimate.

Emotionally intimate.

There was an unguardedness in the way Bex met Faith's eyes, the way she touched her, the way she made her feel good, that made Faith consider how very little of that she'd experienced in her life.

Her thoughts contrasted with the way her body felt, ratcheting up until she wasn't sure if there was anything of her, Faith, left. Or whether her whole world had shrunk down to the places where their skin touched.

Bex's cheeks were soft against Faith's thighs as she licked her, and she wanted to say something, wanted to have that touching her, but she didn't know how. She didn't have any words left in her.

Instead she keened and gasped as her pleasure built and built, until she was trembling on the edge for so long she thought she might cry.

"Please," she begged. "*Please.*"

"Please what, pickle?" said Bex, barely lifting her

mouth from Faith's pussy. Her breath ghosted across Faith's skin, making her shiver. Even that was turning her on.

She was so close; so *damn* close, and still nothing was pushing her over the edge.

"I… I…" Bex was still touching her, her tongue tracing lazy circles around Faith's clit that had her legs trembling. "I need you to fill me up."

The heat in Bex's eyes was almost enough to send her over the edge on its own. "Say please."

"I already said please," she muttered and glared.

That made Bex laugh, and she shifted so that she could slide inside Faith.

Two fingers, gliding in so smoothly, Faith was just that wet. The sound she made was guttural, and then Bex started moving her fingers. Not pumping in and out, like Faith would have expected, but inside. Stroking forward until she hit the bump that was Faith's g-spot.

Fucking hell that felt good.

Real fucking good.

"Is that enough?" Bex asked. "Or do you want *more*?" She added a third finger with that last word, and Faith groaned.

"Almost there, I'm almost there." She didn't know what it was she needed to tip over, but she was so desperate for it she might start crying if it didn't happen soon.

"Look at me." Bex had shifted so that her body was above Faith's, her fingers buried inside her. "Look at me, Faith."

She looked.

"You can do this. I've got you." And finally, she added, "You're mine."

And Faith came so hard she started crying.

CHAPTER Eleven

Bex could tell Faith had been desperate, but it had felt like nothing she was doing was going to quite get her there. And so she'd gotten her to stop and focus on Bex.

When Faith had come, Bex had felt a flood of possessiveness that almost alarmed her. She wasn't usually a possessive kind of person. Banging her chest caveman style and claiming her woman wasn't exactly something she did.

It had always felt odd, as if those who did it were trying a little too hard to convince themselves they were in charge.

But the change that had come over Faith when she'd said those two words had been instant. One second, she'd been teetering on the brink of an orgasm, and the next she was coming in Bex's arms.

Faith had needed to hear those words. She'd needed to hear there was someone who had her back, someone who cared.

Someone who'd be there.

Fuck. This was getting complicated fast, and they hadn't even known each other twenty-four hours.

That didn't matter. Because Bex knew, deep down that Faith was hers, they were made for each other in a way she'd only read about in books.

All of a sudden, she didn't want to ride Faith's face. She just wanted them to curl up in each other's arms and hold one another.

That hadn't been what she'd expected from this evening—although none of this was what she'd expected from this evening.

Faith sat up then and cupped Bex's face. "Hey," she said softly. "Where'd you go?"

"I'm right here," said Bex, and she kind of was. She still felt awkward about the fact she'd said Faith could go down on her, and now that felt like such a huge risk she wasn't sure if she could bear it.

"Faith, do you mind if we just cuddled?"

Faith looked slightly disappointed but hid her reaction as quickly as she could—the sweetheart. "Of course, I don't mind. We can cuddle away."

"Please," said Bex, who didn't think that she'd be able to keep it together whilst sitting on Faith's face. "I know I said… but…."

"Bex," said Faith, quietly. "It's totally okay. Come here." And it was Bex curling up next to Faith, snuggling close in Faith's arms, rather than the other way around.

It wasn't that Bex wasn't being the Domme, it was just that she was allowing herself to ask for the things she needed.

She couldn't remember the last time she'd done that.

She must have drifted off, because when she awoke, there was a blanket over her, and a very naked Faith snuggling around her.

Bex had a lot more experience being the big spoon than the little spoon, but it was certainly a position she could get used to. Faith's breasts pressed up against her back and she could feel the heat of Faith's pussy against her arse.

Her fingers were shaky as she blinked and surveyed the room. Faith must have turned the lights off because the room was in darkness. It was peaceful, and though her room was just downstairs, Bex decided to just let herself drift off to sleep once more.

The next time she woke, it was less peaceful.

Faith had gotten out of bed and was doing something around the corner that involved some slight banging. What on earth was she doing?

"Morning," croaked Bex. "Gods, what time is it?"

"It's gone ten," said Faith. "I didn't expect us to sleep in so late!"

"I suppose we did go to bed late," said Bex, getting out of bed and giving a good stretch. "The Dungeon didn't open 'til nine, and we must have been... well, *you know*... until at least midnight." She padded around the corner until she saw what Faith was up to.

"I forget how time flies when you're having fun," said Faith, with a cheeky grin over her shoulder. "I think we missed breakfast, but there are some ingredients in the fridge here, so I'm making pancakes." She looked down at the pan and amended her statement. "I'm *attempting* to make pancakes. They're a bit gloopy."

She wasn't wrong, although they were also pink, which was very cute.

"Raspberries," explained Faith when Bex pointed this out. "There was a container in the fridge and it seemed a shame to waste them."

"Yum," said Bex. "I'll take gloopy pancake raspberries." She looked guiltily at Faith. "I have to admit that my post-coital food provision usually extends to really nice sandwiches, and maybe a cooked breakfast if I've got all the bits in for it. I'm not the best of cooks, so whatever you're doing will be far far better than what I can give you in return."

Faith smiled shyly at that. "Do you mean you think this'll happen again?"

Bex didn't quite know what to make of that. "I mean, I'd absolutely love it, only if you're not sure..."

"No, no," Faith protested. "I would love to as well; I just wasn't sure if you wanted to."

Bex clocked what Faith was referring to and sighed internally. But she liked Faith too much not to explain, even if the mere idea of it was enough to have her break out in hives. "I just felt really exposed. Unsure of myself for a second and realized that I needed physical comfort more than I needed physical pleasure in that moment."

"I see." Faith nodded and flipped the pancakes. "I think that makes sense, and it was—of course—totally okay to do that. I just wanted to check in with you about it."

Bex came up behind her and kissed Faith's neck. "Thank you. You're beyond sweet."

Faith served up the pancakes, and they sat at the little table by the kitchenette to eat.

"Would you like to spend the day with me today?" asked Bex. She wasn't sure exactly what they'd do—maybe go for a walk, maybe explore some more of the Rawhide Ranch grounds—but she knew that whatever she was going to do this weekend, she wanted to do it with Faith.

"That sounds lovely," said Faith. "Yes please."

CHAPTER Twelve

After breakfast, Bex said she should probably head back to her room to shower and change, and that she'd reconvene with Faith in the main lobby at midday.

"I've got a seedling of a plan for our date day," she said. "Are you okay with me surprising you?"

Faith was absolutely fine with that.

Her experience with relationships had mainly been limited to the odd one-night stand, or an interaction at a club. You'd think that being a potter, there'd have been plenty of lovely gay girls coming through her work place who'd have asked her out, but it had somehow never really happened.

It was, Faith supposed, rather difficult to ask someone out when they—or you—were at work. That had always felt like it was crossing some kind of unspoken line. One of the rules neurotypicals had, but never quite explained. And she knew there were circumstances where it would have just been downright inappropriate, so in the end, she'd just given up and focused on work instead.

She had a social life. She had friends. She just didn't have a partner.

And now here was Bex, who intended on spending her entire morning planning a day out for the two of them.

Mandi looked slightly bemused when Faith explained this to her. "No offense, Faith, but that's a bit of a low bar—*no,* Tommy, we *don't* throw books."

The Little boy looked guiltily over to her. "Sorry, Miss Mandi," he said, carefully picking the book up and putting it back where it belonged. "I won't do it again."

"I should hope not," said Mandi, and then twinkled a smile at Faith. "He's not a bad boy," she whispered. "But he gets lonely and wants attention, bless him." They were spending the morning together in the Littles' Library, and it was really fascinating to see Mandi in her Big headspace. It was a real contrast, hearing all the other Littles call her Miss Mandi, and see how very good she was at her job.

Even her dynamic with Amelia was slightly different while they were working. Mandi still called Amelia Mommy, but their interactions were limited to affectionate professionalism.

Faith had never really seen kinky couples outside of their kink dynamics, and it made her consider how she'd want her and Bex to work.

If they were going to be something… more, that was.

When Mandi had her break, she pulled Faith into Amelia's office—demanding, "Mommy, you need to leave so Faith and I can talk about grown-up things" to Amelia's visible amusement—and asked to hear all about it.

There were so many things to talk about, but Faith found it wasn't the sex or the kink that the conversation gravitated to, but how she felt about it all.

"You remember how much of a wreck I was when you first met me, don't you?"

Mandi looked a bit taken aback. "You weren't a wreck, you were just a bit sad and lonely."

Faith rolled her eyes. "Fine, sad and lonely. The problem is that when I'm with Bex, I don't feel sad or lonely."

"I'm sorry, I don't know what the problem is," said Mandi. "Surely not feeling sad and lonely is a good thing?"

Taking a shaky breath, Faith tried to explain. "I've known her for twenty-four hours, maybe less. How can I possibly feel this comfortable with her already? What if that's just my ADHD part of my AuDHD getting all excited? That I'm not actually into her, and this is just dopamine because someone is showing me some attention for the first time. Or maybe the sex and the kink are so great that I'm ignoring any issues." She could hear her voice getting a little higher pitched panicky. "I don't know what I'm doing, Mandi. And my biggest fear is that all these anxieties will sabotage this before it even starts."

Mandi looked very serious. "Our brains are different from other people's, and I can see how that might make you worried about how that might impact the way you view this… relationship?"

The word relationship felt like a clang. It wasn't fair. Faith had been so excited about the prospect of spending the day with Bex, and now she was all shaky nerves. The in-breath she took was jagged, and she closed her eyes and focused on trying to self-regulate so she didn't slip into a panic attack.

"Hey." Mandi sounded sympathetic. "I get it, I really do. Especially as someone who has been in a relationship with someone whose red flags I *did* ignore—not Mommy Amelia, obviously. But it's very easy to elevate nice actions into wonderful actions after moments like that. So here's what I'm going to say to you: this day-date plan sounds lovely, but it's the minimum of what you should expect. So go, have a great time, but remember this is what you should be getting on the regular—someone who considers you."

"Someone who considers me." That was a way of thinking about it that hadn't occurred to Faith before. "So I should go today?"

"If you want to, absolutely. All you can do is listen to your gut and try not to let the brain snakes hiss in your ear and freak you out. And if you're unsure, you can always chat to me or Amelia about it."

"That'd be amazing, thank you," said Faith.

"And remember that Rawhide does extensive background checks on people, so that's an extra layer of protection. Security guards are all over the site, and you can always go and ask any of the staff for help if you need it. We're a friendly bunch."

As she walked down to join Bex in reception for their date day at midday, Faith ran through everything Mandi had said. It was difficult, not having a model from which she could base her interactions. She couldn't even use her parents as she'd never known her mom, and her dad had never remarried. He, much like Faith, had spent his life dedicated to his art, and so didn't prioritize time with other people. Even his relationship with Faith had been based around the creation of art.

It meant she'd gotten so used to being on her own, hyper independent, that even her friends were held at a slight distance. She never felt like she knew anyone well enough to let down her walls, in case she messed up, and it was only now that Faith was truly realizing how much that had held her up.

By the time she reached the lobby, she was feeling slightly panicky, and Bex took one look at her face and drew her over to one of the seating areas and sat her down. She'd changed into khakis and a shirt with the sleeves rolled up that at any other moment would have flustered Faith, but right now she was just focusing on breathing.

"What's going on, pickle?" asked Bex, and it was the

pet name that pulled Faith back from the brink and made her calm down slightly.

"I'm really worried," she said, the words coming out in a jumbled mess. "That I'm not going to be very good at this. I've never had a proper relationship before, and you're just… well… you're just the best thing ever, and I'm terrified I'm going to fuck it up before we've even started."

Bex sighed and leaned back on the couch.

Fuck. She'd fucked it all up already. Faith's eyes burned and she fought not to cry.

"I'm terrified too."

"Wait, what?"

Bex ran her hand through her hair, ruffling it up. "I've slept with plenty of people, but my relationships have never lasted very long, or been particular successes. It's not that I'm bad at it, I've just never been particularly good at it."

"Seriously?"

"Seriously." She even looked relieved, as if it had been stressing her out too. "I have no idea what I'm doing, so I've gone for a classic. It's summer, the weather's nice, there's a lake over by the Big House, so I thought we'd go have a picnic. That way we can hang out, chat, and get to know each other better. I didn't think there'd be any way I could fuck up a picnic. Especially as I got the kitchen to make one up, so I didn't accidentally give you food poisoning."

Faith blinked. "Have we both been panicking?"

"Are you kidding? I've been in a state of gay panic ever since we met."

That was a little reassuring. Faith started laughing. "Why are we like this?"

"I think it's one of the things they dole out alongside

the gayness," said Bex. "Look, why don't we agree that if we're having a proper panic over something, we'll tell each other? That way we can stave off any panic at the root."

"Okay," said Faith. "Let's try that. Now, you said something about a picnic?"

Chapter Thirteen

They'd taken one of the golf carts over to the large lake, and there was a boat tied up there, with a note saying *For Bex and Faith*.

Bex pointed across the lake where a picnic blanket had been set up beneath the shade of a large tree. "I think that's our picnic."

"Cool!" Faith seemed like she'd gotten back to her bubbly self. The two of them wobbled as they got into the boat. The toe of Bex's shoe caught on the seat in the bow and her arms windmilled wildly. Bex tried to ignore the fact that Faith was looking on in horror as she fought against either capsizing the boat or tumbling into the water. It was a very close call, but finally Bex sat down solidly on the stern seat and took a huge breath.

"Fucking hell. Okay, so lunch is over the other side of the lake. Now, our mission, should you wish to accept it, is to get there."

Faith giggled. "That's okay, we can row across."

"Yes," said Bex. "We definitely can." She had never rowed a day in her life. When planning the picnic, she'd asked Tay what they thought would work, and Tay had suggested this. There had been no mention of a boat, or the need for rowing. As had been apparent when she'd stepped in the boat, Bex was made for dry land.

She stared at the oars, as if that would browbeat them into submission.

"Do you want me to…?"

"No no," said Bex airily, sounding for all the world as if she'd coxed for Cambridge. "I've got this."

It soon became very apparent she did *not* have this.

They started out strong, but at some point, her left

arm started aching and so she let up. Big mistake. They started going round and round in circles.

Faith was very sweet about the whole thing, and didn't even offer to help, though Bex could tell that she wanted to. But after about ten minutes of making swirly patterns on the lake's surface, she gave up and looking pleadingly at Faith. "Help?"

"Of course." She didn't tease Bex either, but just talked through what she was doing as they moved toward the waiting picnic quickly. "You can take us back after," she said. "You'll have it down by then."

They managed to get out of the boat without overturning it, and Bex was very grateful when her feet hit the soil on the bank. "Finally," she said, jokingly getting to her knees and kissing the earth. "I never thought we'd make it."

They both laughed, and Faith threw herself onto the picnic blanket, whilst Bex clambered over to join her.

Tay and the kitchen team had done an incredible job. They'd picked a shady spot so the picnickers didn't burn in the midday sun. August in Montana was actually cooler than in the UK, but Bex wore sunscreen year-round because she was prone to burning. A spot in the shade was definitely for the best.

The blanket was laid out with cushions for them to sit on, and the biggest picnic hamper Bex had ever seen sat in place of pride at the center. Made of wicker, it looked exactly what Bex thought a picnic basket should look like, promising edible treats.

Opening it revealed a treasure trove of Italian picnic goodies. Cured meats and cheeses, pickled vegetables, sundried tomatoes, and an assortment of dips and accompanying crudités. Faith's eyes got wide in that way they did when she was excited. Bex was starting to recognize that look.

There was a flask with iced peach tea which Bex poured out into glasses for them, and then they started eating. The flavors were paired together really well, the sweetness of the pickled vegetables marrying perfectly with the acidity of the sundried tomatoes, and the creaminess of the cheese. It was a masterful picnic, and far superior to anything Bex would have been able to put together herself.

There was silence for a good while whilst the two of them dug in, with just the occasional hum of happiness as they ate.

It was a comfortable silence, and Bex was pleased to note Faith was as invested in the picnic as she was, so they didn't have to fuck about with small talk when they'd rather be eating.

Eventually, they finished, leaned back and sighed in unison.

"You were hungry," said Bex.

"So were you," said Faith.

"Well, we worked up quite the appetite last night, I suppose," said Bex, teasingly.

Faith blushed and threw a grissini at her. "Oh, hush you. I thought we were supposed to be getting to know each other, not getting horny again."

"We can't do both?" Bex was joking though, and she smiled to soften her words. After taking a bite of the thrown Italian breadstick, she pointed it at Faith. "Okay, tell me about you, Faith. Why pottery?"

A look came over Faith's face that wasn't dissimilar to the one Bex had seen when Faith had started slipping into subspace. It spoke of peace and happiness. "Are you actually interested? Because it's my special interest and a lot of people get really bored when I start talking about it."

"That sounds rude," said Bex.

"Oh no," said Faith. "I'm quite capable of rabbit holing and accidentally delivering a lecture for an hour if not reined in, so knowing what level of interest you have will help me pitch it."

That sounded exhausting. "Ummm, I want to know why you like it, and if that means you go off one for a bit, I'm totally fine with that."

Faith looked so unsure, but as she started to speak, her confidence began to shine through. "So for me it's a mix of two things. Firstly, it's the ability to create something that's so changeable. You start working in clay, and it's wet and messy, but when you fire it in the oven, it transforms into something else completely. And then when you glaze it, it changes again. Somehow each step of that feels like art to me, different pieces of art while being the same thing all at once. It's incredible."

"It sounds transformative," said Bex.

"Exactly that!" said Faith, her eyes shining. "We run a lot of outreach programs, including some with trans youth. For them, seeing how the same piece can change depending on the treatment can be really illuminating. And they get to take something home that they've transformed, as a reminder that change is possible."

Bex could see that. "That sounds like it would be a real boon for students who are struggling. It's amazing your work does that—that you do that."

"Thank you." Faith blushed. "I helped develop the program; it's one of our most popular ones. We have students coming from all over state, and sometimes from out of state as well. You're new to our Montana, right?"

"I am," said Bex. "Been here about six months, but stuck to the big cities, so it hasn't been too bad for me."

"The big cities are usually okay on general queer rights," said Faith, "but gender identity…" She paused. "We had a lot of complaints about the trans and nonbinary specialist sessions at work. Montana's one of the only states to completely ban drag queens from reading in libraries. And two years ago, the governor tried to ban all gender-affirming care for minors, and it was only halted because the District Court put a stop to it." She took a shuddery breath, and Bex scooted over to give her a hug.

"It's shit," she said. "In the UK, they've currently got a complete ban on puberty blockers for minors in place, and in our queer communities, we've seen the impact the ban is having. There are trans children who'll never get to grow up, never get to live full lives as their true selves because they can't bear their current existence." Bex's eyes filled with tears and she angrily dashed them away. "Fuck. Thank you for creating a safe space for those kids; that's everything."

Faith nodded. "It's one of the reasons why I was okay with coming here. When I spoke to Mandi about visiting, she talked about Tay. Knowing that Rawhide Ranch is fully inclusive means everything. It means we can be ourselves and be safe. That's not a gift everyone has. I do miss being able to work with clay though. I usually do some work every day."

"You said there were two main reasons why pottery."

"Yes, the other is that my brain quiets when I'm working. I stop worrying about life and my day-to day-stuff, because I have to focus on what I'm making or the wheel will destroy it. My brain quieting isn't something that happens all that often, so I value it when it does."

She shot a look up at Bex. "Flogging does that too. I really love that."

Bex leaned down and kissed her. "I can see how that would be amazing. Anything you want to know about me?"

"So what brought you to the US?" asked Faith.

Bex had been expecting the question but hadn't really considered what she'd say when the subject was broached. At work, she usually muttered something about a love for travel, but she didn't want to use an answer she knew by rote with Faith—especially when it wasn't strictly true.

"My dad died last year," she said, her voice completely level. She didn't need sympathy, but braced herself for it, just in case it was offered.

CHAPTER Fourteen

Oh shit. Faith knew there were very strict rules about how you were supposed to respond when someone said a parent had died, but when she looked at Bex, Bex looked like she didn't really want to talk about it.

Even though Bex was opening up, Faith could feel something coming up between them.

She decided to be honest. "Look, death is shit, but I never really understand if me telling you something you already know helps at all. So, I'm sorry for your pain. Is that okay to say?"

Bex smiled and huffed out a laugh. "Yeah, that is definitely okay to say, pickle. And I know what you mean. It always feels like people are being sympathetic to ease their own guilty consciences—or maybe that's just my family."

"Ah," said Faith.

"Yeah. Dad died and all of sudden they started coming out of the woodwork, keen to help me sort through all of his stuff when they couldn't be arsed to come and visit him in the two years leading up to it. It had all been on my shoulders, not—" she added fervently, "that I ever begrudged him that. It had always just been me and Dad, and I wasn't going to let him down." There was a pause, as if Bex was working out what to say next. "I mean, they're family, and everyone kept telling me that I needed to be more understanding. Only they hadn't been there. They hadn't given a crap about Dad when he was alive, so why would he give a crap about them in death?" Her face set, hard, as if she was bracing herself for criticism. "So I dealt with all the legal stuff, pointed out that no they *weren't* entitled to anything just because they were blood relatives, and then I left."

Bex looked haunted.

"That must have been difficult."

"I mean, yes and no. Dad had always been home for me. When he wasn't there anymore, it was harder to stay. It felt wrong without him. But I sold the place, because it would have felt more wrong seeing them there, when they'd never bothered visiting whilst he was alive." She swallowed and forced a smile. "You're getting all the emotion from me today."

"Is that okay?" asked Faith. "I don't want you to do anything you're not comfortable with." These were big emotional feelings and she didn't know how best to support Bex. Usually that would have sent her into a bit of a spiral, but with Bex, she knew all she had to do was ask. "What do you need?"

Bex looked startled at the questions. "It's weird, but somehow I'm okay talking about it with you—more so than even with my best friend. And as for need? Well, I could do with a hug?"

Faith was more than happy to oblige with that. It turned out that the two of them slot together perfectly, as if they'd been made to fit next to each other. She shifted so that she leant back against the trunk of the tree whose shade they sat in and lifted her arm.

Bex scooted over and snuggled up to her, her head fitting in the hollow below her chin.

Comfortable silence ensued.

Too often, silence felt weighted, like there was something she was supposed to be doing that she'd missed, but that wasn't the case with Bex. With Bex, silence was just that, silence.

Her gaze fell upon a bag packed into the picnic basket, and she reached over to grab it. "What's this?"

Bex turned her head to look. "I'm not sure. Tay must have put it in there."

It was a fairly heavy bag, and when she opened it, there was a note from Mandi.

I know you can't use your potter's wheel while you're here, but maybe you and Bex can play with these paints instead? - Mandi

The thoughtful note made Faith smile, and she peeked in the bag to see what Mandi had packed for her. There was a collection of paint pots, all different colors, and so many of them Faith could have painted a rainbow made up of slightly different hues many times over.

"What's that?" asked Bex.

"Paint," said Faith. "Mandi suggests that we play with some paint."

Bex got a thoughtful look upon her face. "Hmmmm… paint?"

"What?" There was something mischievous about the brunette's smile, and Faith wasn't entirely certain what was in store for her.

"Well, I have an idea, but we'd need to ask someone at the Ranch to set it up for us. You trust me?"

Faith looked at Bex. The other woman had softened in her arms, and though she was the Top, there was a levelness between them both, neither of them having more power over the other. A balance Faith had never really felt with a Domme before. "Yes," she said.

Making it back across the lake, the boat laden down with all of the remnants of picnic was super fun. Bex was determined to make it across and make it she did, even if by the end she was swearing pretty much continuously at the oars. Faith couldn't hide her amusement, and by the time they tied up the boat after climbing out, the two of them were practically belly laughing.

"I swear," said Bex, "that next time I organize a date, I will ensure that we don't have to fucking row *anywhere*."

"I don't know," said Faith. "I'd kind of like to take you out on one of our large Montana lakes."

The look Bex shot her was one of absolute incredulity.

"I'm joking." Faith laughed, bending over to alleviate the stitch she'd developed. "I'm joking, I'm joking. I promise."

"Damn straight you are," said Bex, shaking her head. "Fucking lakes. Absolute lunacy."

CHAPTER Fifteen

Driving back to the main Rawhide Ranch building in the golf cart was lovely. The weather was idyllic—sunny, but not too hot, with a breeze that made the whole experience really very pleasant. When they pulled up, Bex leaned over and kissed Faith. "So my plan involves some playtime, if you're up for that?"

Faith's eyebrows rose. "Oh yes?"

"Oh yes." Bex leaned forward until their noses kissed. "I can't wait to get you naked and play with you some more." She felt Faith shiver at her words and smiled wolfishly. "I need an hour to set it up. Meet me back in the lobby then?"

Her girl nodded in agreement.

"Oh, I was planning on using one of the private playrooms. You okay with that?"

"As long as it's just us, yeah."

"Just us," promised Bex, and stole another kiss, before leaving Faith on the porch and driving the golf cart back down the drive.

Her plan involved finding the perfect branch.

Spotting a familiar figure, Bex slowed the cart and pulled to a stop beside Luna who'd been walking across the drive. Once she explained a bit of her plan, Luna smiled and nodded.

"Continue driving down that way and you'll come across one of our gardens. I'll have our head landscaper meet you there."

"Thank you," Bex said. It didn't take long before she rounded a bend in the drive and knew she'd found the garden. Lush blooms and verdant greenery spread out before her. She stopped the golf cart a few feet away from a man who'd stepped out to greet her.

"Bex?" With her nod, he continued, "It's a pleasure to meet you. I'm Lucas Morrow. Luna said you'd like some help?"

"It's a bit of an odd request," Bex said, flushing for the first time in a long time. How to explain her idea? "I need a branch. Nothing that's going to sting too much, but has some flex and give in it. I'd rather not break one off a tree though, so if you know of a place that might have branches scattered across the ground…?"

The tanned man ran his hand over his head and looked thoughtful. "For a branch like that, I think we're looking at the aspens. It's summer, so finding one on the ground might be a bit tricky, but come on, let's see what there is."

Joining her in the cart, he gave her directions which led her across a green field toward a thicket of trees.

Bex didn't know all that much about trees. She knew a little about elms, considering Brighton back home was the custodian of the National Elm Collection. One of her friends had made trees their special interest and Bex was able to recall that there were over 125 different types of elms in Brighton alone—more than anywhere else in the world.

But trees in general? Not her specialty.

These trees though? Even Bex could tell that they were special.

They had spindly silver trunks, with the bark bursting out in dark lines—just like the marks from a cane on a submissive's skin. Taller than almost any tree she'd seen before, they towered above her, green leaves dancing on the wind.

"These are quaking aspens," said Lucas. "They've

got the flex you want; now we just need to find a branch."

Bex stared up at the leaves bobbing on the breeze. One floated down, and she caught it in her hand. "It's shaped like a heart!" she said, delightedly.

"Yes, that is rather lovely," said Lucas. "Oh, over here!"

The perfect branch was nestled at the foot of a few trees. It was long, but felt right in Bex's hand, and made a very satisfying swish when she brought it down through the air.

"That'll work well enough?"

"It's perfect," she said. "Thank you, Lucas."

Carting said branch through the lobby got some raised eyebrows, and when she'd explained to Luna exactly why she needed it, Luna had grinned. As Bex approached the desk, Luna picked up the phone and called the Dungeon security guard from the previous day up to the check-in desk.

"Drake, could you take this branch and this bag down to private playroom six please? And it needs to be set up like this." She outlined Bex's plan and Drake looked impressed.

"Wow, is this for you and your lady from last night?"

"Yeah, it is," said Bex, grinning widely. "She's going to absolutely love it. I said that I'd have it all set up in an hour, which is in about half an hour—is that doable?"

"Absolutely," said Drake. "Leave it with me."

As they were talking, a tall man came out of the office by the check-in desk.

"Hi, Master Derek," said Luna.

"Mr. Hawkins," said Bex, offering him her hand. "So nice to meet you."

"Most people call me Master Derek," smiled Derek,

and chuckled at the expression on her face. As if knowing the Domme had no intention of referring to anyone as Master, but also had no intention of being rude either, he assured her, "Mr. Hawkins is just fine though. How're you finding your stay? You said it's your first time at a play space here in the US?"

"That's right," she said. "My best friend—who was my reference, I believe—owns a club back home, and I'd been missing some playtime. Your staff are incredibly accommodating. Rawhide is one of the best run places I've ever seen, and the amenities are genuinely excellent. I'll definitely be coming back for longer than a weekend visit."

"We'd be delighted to have you," he said. "I believe you've been spending quite a bit of time with Ms. Faith."

She met his gaze head-on. "Yes, that's right."

He didn't say very much, just looked at her, and Bex had the uncanny feeling he was seeing right to the center of her feelings for Faith. "That sounds like it could be a really beneficial experience for the two of you."

And despite the fact she knew he was checking her over and making sure her intentions were good, she couldn't help beaming at him. "She's amazing."

Derek Hawkins smiled back. "I'm glad. Sometimes we find that person who just completes us, and those beneficial experiences can transform us."

"Transformation seems to be the word of the day." She just shook her head when he looked at her questioningly. "Luna and Drake have been amazing in setting up quite a complicated scene for us, so I'm very grateful."

Luna merely waved away her thanks. "Just doing my job," she said.

"And you're very good at it," her boss said. "Can you

send Sadie in to see me when she comes down from the Littles' Wing?"

"Absolutely, Master Derek."

"I'm going to grab a drink from the café," said Bex. "And wait for Faith. Nice to meet you."

"Nice to meet you too," he said.

As it was after the lunch rush, the café was pretty quiet, and Bex grabbed a coffee and sat down at a table. She was looking forward to the scene, definitely, but she just needed a minute to prepare herself. Creating a scene like this, which was so personal to the person subbing, wasn't something she'd done in this way before, and Bex found that she was nervous.

She wanted Faith to more than like it. She wanted Faith to *love* it, and if she didn't, then Bex would feel like she'd misread everything completely.

She thought back to the conversation they'd had by the lake about her dad and home. And she thought back to that feeling, that knowledge she'd had, that Faith was her home.

How did you tell someone that?

How did you go up to someone you'd known less than forty-eight hours and tell them that, hey, this was it for you? That you'd found your person, and that person was them.

Her phone buzzed in her pocket and she looked down to see a text from Riley.

Hope you're having fun with your cowgirl. And it's okay. You can visit.

Even her best friend seemed to sense it, to sense the fact something was fundamentally different.

Bex didn't know how to respond, because she knew this was Riley's way of letting her know that if Bex stayed in America, it was fine because she'd know it was because her best friend had finally found true happiness. Too moved to answer, Bex just slid the phone back into her pocket with a smile.

She looked out of the doors of the café and saw Faith waiting for her in the lobby. She was wearing a jumpsuit, and when Bex saw the ribbon that held it up, her heart skipped a beat. Untie that and the material would fall in a puddle at Faith's feet.

Gods she was crazy about this woman.

CHAPTER Sixteen

Bex hadn't changed since the picnic, but she had put her hair up into a ponytail, and as they walked toward the elevator together, Faith watched, fascinated, as it swung back and forth.

"What?" asked Bex, looking bemused.

"I like your ponytail," said Faith.

"Thanks," said Bex. "I need my hair up and out of the way for our scene this afternoon. I wanted to do it now before the Dungeon closes for cleaning at seven. That way we can have dinner and watch a movie together tonight. Finish off our date day together—if that's okay, of course. I don't know if you had other plans…?"

"I don't," said Faith. She'd spoken to Mandi about the date day, and they'd agreed to have lunch together on Sunday before Faith left for home. "I'm having lunch with Mandi tomorrow, but I spent all day with her yesterday, and a couple of hours with her today. I'm all yours tonight." The words sounded like a promise, and they kind of were.

This time, taking the elevator down to the Dungeon, both of them were less nervous. There was a frisson of excitement in the air, and Faith held Bex's hand, smiling in anticipation for what was to come.

The same security guard was on the entrance to the Dungeon, and he grinned at them both. "All set up for you, Bex."

"Thanks, Drake." She grinned at him.

Faith looked between them and furrowed her brow. "What's set up?"

"Patience," chided Bex, leading them through the

main play space down toward the private playrooms. It was a different one from the room they'd used the night before, and Bex paused before she opened the door.

"Look, it may look really weird, the way it's set up, but I promise you there's a good reason for it."

"Okaaaaay," said Faith, unsure of what to suspect.

When the door opened, the room beyond looked very odd indeed. It was clearly usually a wet room of some kind, but plastic sheeting had been taped to the walls, and when she looked up, she saw it was on the ceiling as well.

"I think," said Faith, trying very hard not to burst into hysterical laughter, "you'd better explain what sort of scene you have planned that's turned this room into something out of a true-crime documentary on serial killers."

Bex's mouth dropped open. "Fuck, I didn't think of that. Shit, Faith, I promise you, it's nothing like that."

"Well, considering Drake helped set it up, I should think not. What *is* going on?"

Bex walked over to a plastic-covered table and drew back a cloth to reveal the paint pots Mandi had put into the picnic basket.

Oh. Paint. The weird room set up made sense now. Well, sort of.

"I don't quite see why the entire room had to be almost vacuum packed though," Faith said, a perplexed look on her face despite the teasing tone in her voice.

"Because," said Bex, with a nervous smile. "I'm going to turn you into art."

Surely she hadn't heard correctly. "What?"

Bex didn't answer immediately. Instead she bustled around Faith, moving frenetically around the room, and Faith realized quite how nervous the other woman was.

Faith tried again. "Ummm, how exactly are you going to do that? Turn me into art, I mean?"

"So I was thinking, I got this branch—see it's super pretty, the leaves are all shaped like hearts—and I thought that if we covered it in paint, I could flog you with it."

"Flog me?"

"Lucas helped me find it."

"Lucas?" Faith didn't know how much she liked the idea of Bex discussing their scene with other people, though she imagined that she'd have had to, to get the play room set up like this.

"He's Rawhide's head landscaper," explained Bex, and then she caught sight of Faith's face. "Oh no, pickle, he didn't have all the details. I just said that I wanted something with flex. Look." She brought over the silvery branch so Faith could get a closer look at it. "It's aspen, so it wouldn't be too stingy—not like a cane, I remember you didn't like the look of those—and the leaves would soften it even more. But I was thinking that I could use it on your back and shoulders and arse—carefully of course—and you could be the canvas. You've been missing your art, but I wanted to show you that you *are* your art. And to turn you into art to prove that."

Faith was speechless. The idea was, well the idea was fucking fantastic. Hot and creative and so *her*. Bex had seen her, truly seen her, and come up with this incredible plan for them both.

"I love it," she said eventually, and threw herself into Bex's arms to kiss her. "It's amazing, perfect. I don't know how you managed to come up with such a clever idea!"

Bex beamed. "You really like it? I'm so sorry about

the serial-killer vibes, I just didn't want to get paint over everything. Well, over everything that's not you."

"I really do." Faith skipped over to the table and examined all the different paints. "How do you want to paint the branch?"

"As I see it," said Bex, "we've got two options: either dip them in the paint pots or use the paintbrushes Mandi gave us to flick paint over it."

"Let's do both," suggested Faith. She could see how it was all going to turn out in her mind's eye, and her fingers started itching to touch the materials. "Dip the branches without leaves on, and flick paint at the leaves —though we'll have to cover them quite a lot to get those heart-shaped prints."

"Excellent!" said Bex. "Come on then, strip off. We'll do this bit in knickers only, and then take those off when I'm flogging you with the branch."

Faith didn't need telling twice, she stripped quickly, almost racing Bex, and then folded all their clothes neatly and placed them under one of the sheets so they wouldn't get paint on them.

Bex brought the branch over, and the two of them took the lids off all the paint pots. Faith found herself stimming excitedly, her fingers dancing all across the paint, dipping in and out of the pots. She laughed, and Bex looked at her with a question in her eyes. "It's not quite the same as working with clay, but the physicality of pottery is one of the things I love about it most, so this is amazing."

"Ever done the *Ghost* thing and had a sexy pottery scene?" Bex asked.

"Not yet," she replied, winking suggestively. "But somehow I think that when you visit my studio, that may change."

Bex looked delighted at that, and Faith felt a warmth spread through her, and only part of it was due to the paint. She was aiming a large paintbrush at the leaves and splattering it with thick paint, and impetuously she aimed it in Bex's direction and got a huge spot of green paint on her breast.

"You're going to pay for that," said Bex.

"Promises, promises," laughed Faith, and then got chased round the room with a paintbrush.

When Bex finally caught her, she took the paintbrush and traced a line from Faith's forehead down her nose, skipping her lips, and then down her throat, neck and between her breasts. By the time she paused, just above the elastic of Faith's underwear, Faith was panting.

"Come on," said Bex, as if she'd done nothing at all. "We've got to prep this branch."

They moved quickly, so it didn't dry, and the branch was a kaleidoscope of color by the time Faith took up her position against the wall.

Bex came close and whispered in her ear. "You make the most beautiful canvas I've ever seen."

And Faith shuddered with happiness even as she braced herself.

CHAPTER Seventeen

This was the most fun Bex had ever had in a scene. The two of them were covered in paint, and she was glad Drake had shielded every possible surface in sheets of plastic because what hadn't gone on themselves or the branch appeared to have gone on the walls.

And she was going to get more on there now.

Faith had taken off her lingerie, and was leaning against the wall, facing forward so that paint wouldn't get in her eyes.

They were going to have to have a shower after this.

Bex drew her arm back and let fly. The branch landed with the most satisfying smack on Faith's arse. She pulled it back carefully, trying not to tear any of the leaves. There were a couple of really pretty hearts, but she hadn't realized how attractive the individual twigs on the branches were going to look. Multicolored stripes that followed the pattern of the wood decorated Faith's backside. Damn if that didn't look adorable. This was a great idea.

She wasn't the person who needed to okay it though. "How was that?" Bex asked.

"Not too stingy," said Faith. "You can probably go a bit harder if you like, and I'll watermelon out if I need to."

Those fruit safe words, Gods her girl was the cutest thing ever.

"How are you feeling about your back and shoulders?"

Faith considered the questions. "Slightly less than that would be perfect, and avoid my kidneys?"

"Of course." Bex leaned forward and kissed her cheek. "You look incredible."

"But," said Faith, and she let out a sigh that sounded contented. "But it feels… it feels good, Bex. It feels right."

"Good," said Bex, unable to speak the words that caught on her tongue. *Of course, it feels right. Everything about this—about us—feels right.*

Each strike added an extra layer to the art, until Faith was a mass of color from her shoulders to the bottom of her arse—partly from the paint, and partly reddened from the branch itself.

Bex didn't know if she'd ever seen a sight so beautiful.

Stripes decorated Faith's skin, all jumbled up in a confusion of color that just shouted vibrancy. Heart shapes peeked through where the leaves had caught and printed on the living canvas.

Breathtaking.

"You were made to be art, rainbow girl," said Bex.

"Can you take a photo of me?" asked Faith. "I know that photography's not usually allowed…"

Bex wasn't sure about leaving Faith alone like this, even for just a moment or two, but rules were rules, and Rawhide Ranch was strict about this one. Far better to ask permission, than break the rule and risk a ban. "I can go and ask, but only if you're okay waiting like this for me."

"I can do it," said Faith, and Bex saw the way her jaw set in determination.

"Are you sure?" She came up close and spoke her words into Faith's ear. "You'll have to stay very very still for me, rainbow girl. As still as a statue."

The shuddery breath Faith let out told Bex everything she needed to hear. "You've got it," she said. "Wait here; I'll be right back."

Slipping her trousers and shirt on quickly, Bex ran through the Dungeon, ignoring the curious looks at the paint on her face, and poked her head outside the Dungeon doors. Spotting Drake at his podium, she exited and approached him. "Drake, is it possible for Mr. Hawkins to sign off on me taking a photo of Faith? Her back is the canvas, and she wants to see it for herself. It'll just be of her and the wall."

Drake set his book aside and nodded. "I can see why you'd want to keep a record of that. Give me a moment and I'll call and ask."

Bex waited in anticipation, shuffling from foot to foot impatiently as Drake spoke on the phone. "Yes, yes, sir. Yes, I understand." He offered the phone to Bex. "He'd like to speak to you."

"Hello?"

"Ah, Bex, I can absolutely understand the situation, and how it's appropriate for the scene. I'm happy for the photo to be taken, but it must be taken on Faith's phone, and not yours. And nothing to identify where it's been taken please."

"We can do that," said Bex, breathlessly. "I need to go back, if that's okay. I've left Faith in there on her own."

"Go go," said Derek. He sounded amused. "And thank you for checking, Bex. I really do appreciate your respect for our rules."

Bex practically shoved the phone back at Drake and ran back to the playroom as fast as she could.

"Hey there, rainbow girl, you all good?"

"I'm all good," said Faith, but her voice had gone all

floaty, the way it had the night Bex had first flogged her into subspace.

"You are better than good," said Bex. "You are perfect. My perfect rainbow girl."

"Your perfect rainbow girl."

"We've got permission to take a photo of you, but it has to be on your phone. Where's your phone, rainbow girl?"

"Oh, it's in my room. There are rules stating no phones in the Dungeon."

Bex remembered reading that as well. "That's fine. I'll ask Drake to call Mandi and see if she or Tay can get it and bring it to the Dungeon and then wait to take it back upstairs."

Faith gurgled with laughter. "You're running all over the place, aren't you?"

"I'd run to the center of the earth and back for you," said Bex, but she was concerned. Faith seemed light-headed and she didn't want her to fall.

Sticking her head out the door of the playroom, she gestured to one of the service submissives, who hurried over and nodded before going to relay Bex's message to Drake.

Next time she'd plan this better. If there was a next time.

Faith was silent now, swaying slightly on the spot, and Bex came and took her hands, shifting her so that she could meet her rainbow girl's eyes. They were slightly unfocused, and Faith had a dreamy look on her face.

"Are you sure you're okay with me taking a photo of you?"

Faith laughed, the sound airy. "I asked you to, of course I'm okay with it."

Bex took Faith's chin and adjusted the angle of her

face so that their eyes met. "Faith, I need to know you're making that decision with full capacity."

Faith took a deep breath, and it took a moment of blinking before her eyes refocused and the cloud cleared. "I'm sure. And on my phone is a good plan."

That sounded more like Faith's analytical side, so Bex was satisfied with that.

While they waited for Drake to bring them the phone, Bex stroked Faith's hair, trying to anchor her in the scene, so she didn't just float off. As much as seeing her rainbow girl in subspace was adorable, Bex had very definite opinions about making sure people had the capacity to consent—even mid-scene. Luckily, it didn't take too long for Drake to knock on the door and pass the phone through.

"Thank you, I'll be right back," Bex promised.

"Take your time. Make sure you get the perfect shot," Drake said with a grin that was answered by one of her own.

Handing the phone to Faith to unlock and click on the camera icon, Bex checked her over. Faith gave it back with a smile.

"Photograph me, Bex. Because you made me into art. I'm the art."

She stepped back toward the wall, and turned so that the curvature of her body could be seen, the paint on her skin clearly visible.

Bex swallowed. Wow.

"Yes, rainbow girl," said Bex. "You're the most beautiful art that I've ever seen." She wasn't the best photographer in the world, but she tried to recall anything she'd ever heard about composition and lined up the camera so that just the top of Faith's arse was in frame, and then the nape of her neck, with hair curling above the painted skin.

The contrast between the paint and the marks left by the branch seemed even more vivid on camera. Bex wasn't sure if she'd ever seen something so erotic.

Wordlessly, she handed the phone over to Faith, who scrolled through the photos.

Faith didn't say anything either, but a single tear rolled down her cheek.

"Oh, rainbow girl," said Bex, and pulled Faith into her arms, paint be damned.

"Your clothes," protested Faith.

"Fuck my clothes," said Bex. "Why are you crying?"

"Because you made me into art," said Faith. "I know the truth of how I look. There's nothing special about me; I'm just ordinary. But this? With this you've made me extraordinary."

"No," said Bex fiercely. "You have always been extraordinary. You just didn't realize it."

CHAPTER Eighteen

The high from being made into art didn't dissipate as they walked together, hand in hand, back through the Dungeon. The line of paint from Faith's forehead to belly button was accentuated by the plunging neckline of her jumpsuit. Drake spluttered with laughter as he saw her.

"Well, aren't you two a picture?" he said.

"Yes, we are," said Bex. "The perfect picture."

His answering smile acknowledged how happy they both looked.

Faith wasn't sure if he needed to check the photographs, but he waved the phone away when she offered it. "That's between you and Bex. We trust you."

She smiled her relief at him. "Thank you, Drake," Faith said.

"You're very welcome." He smiled at Bex as well, and then returned to reading a different book than before, but Faith was willing to bet it was another romance novel judging by the cover.

"Which floor, rainbow girl?" asked Bex as the elevator doors pinged open and they stepped inside.

"Yours," said Faith firmly. "I want to stay with you tonight."

After the scene they'd had, she wanted to be with Bex.

She *needed* to be with Bex.

"That sounds utterly lush," replied the other woman, and pressed the button for the second floor.

Bex's suite was almost identical to Faith's; in fact, she thought hers might be directly above Bex's. The idea that they'd been arriving and getting ready for their weekend at Rawhide in parallel, one above the other made her feel all warm inside.

"Shower time," said Bex. "We've got to all that paint off you before sit on any fabric furnishings. I don't want to have to pay for those bedsheets to be replaced because I have a feeling they're far more expensive than either of us realize."

The shower was a walk-in, with a rainfall showerhead and was more than big enough for the two of them. There was a bench built in against one wall, Bex and motioned for Faith to sit down.

"Too bad we can't shut that off," said Faith, pointing to the ceiling. "I find rainfall showers a bit overwhelming."

Bex grinned and gestured toward the shower spray wand. "Never fear, I got you covered. Besides, I don't think it'd be possible for a rainfall shower to get all of the paint. I'm going to have to hand wash you, rainbow girl."

Faith sat down on the bench, feeling the cool marble against her tush. She loved how Bex didn't dismiss her needs out of hand. Rainfall showers were a sensory nightmare. She had to keep her eyes clear from the water at all times, or else she'd end up screwing them shut and that was how accidents happened. Before she'd lived in her current apartment, she'd had a showerhead over a bath, instead of a separate walk-in shower, and had fallen over the side of the tub while her eyes were closed more times than was funny.

But she didn't have to do that here, because Bex had adjusted her plans accordingly.

The shower turned on, and Bex aimed the spray at Faith's back. The steady stream hit her, insistent, and as she started to see some of the color swirl down the drain, her mood dipped. She didn't want to not be art anymore.

Lowering her head until her chin hit her chest, she took in some deep breaths. The stream of water stopped and Bex moved around until she was standing in front of Faith. She dropped the wand, and it bounced against the tiles, the noise echoing, but Bex didn't seem to care.

She got down on her knees and looked up at Faith.

"Hey, rainbow girl, what's the matter?"

"If you wash the paint off," said Faith, sniffling a little bit, "I won't be a rainbow girl anymore."

"Oh, pickle," said Bex. "You'll always be my rainbow girl, paint or no paint."

That made logical sense, Faith knew that, but she wasn't feeling very logical right now. Nothing felt logical about any of this.

"Okay," said Bex. "I think you might be experiencing some sub drop. So we've a couple of options here: we can continue with the shower and then get you wrapped up in fluffy towels after; we can wrap you up in fluffy towels now; or we can have some fun time in the shower together. I think all three of those are decent enough options."

Faith looked at her eagerly. "Fun shower times," she said. "As long as I get to pick what we do."

Bex looked wary but nodded. "We can do that."

"Your turn to sit down then!" Faith said and moved Bex to sit exactly as she had been sitting moments ago. And then Faith took up the spot on the floor that Bex had just vacated.

From this angle, she could see all of Bex. The way her full breasts swung slightly, each time she moved, the swell of her belly above her thighs, and that perfectly round face.

"I'd like to taste you, please."

Bex met her eyes, and slowly nodded. "If you're sure?"

"I'm sure," said Faith, and with gentle hands, pushed Bex's knees apart.

Her clit was pretty and a dark pink, as if Bex had been wanting this for a very long time.

"I think you want me," said Faith, and she was delighted when Bex swore.

"Of *course*, I fucking want you. You're my rainbow girl and you're all bouncy and chirpy and naked. You're so very very naked for me and—"

Faith had decided that that was enough talking from Bex, so she leaned forward and sucked on that pretty clit as hard as she could.

"*Fuck.*"

Faith grinned. That one word had been very heartfelt.

It turned out that as sweary as Bex was in day-to-day life, it was nothing compared to what she was like when Faith was eating her out.

And she tasted delicious. A slight tang with a sweetness behind it. Faith could have lost herself in that forever. Could have drowned in it.

Might well drown in it because Bex was wet, dripping over Faith's tongue and then, as she added them, over her fingers too.

She angled her head so she could breathe out of one nostril, a movement that must have made her look a little ridiculous, she was sure, but she must have brushed up against a sensitive spot because Bex groaned. And then hands were in her hair, urging her closer.

Bex began to move against her tongue, riding her

face the way Faith had dreamed of, and the tiles beneath her knees faded away and all there was, was this.

Bex.

Her scent, her taste, her fingers firm against Faith's scalp, almost massaging her as they guided her. Her thighs were either side of Faith's face, thick thighs which felt soft against her skin, and they were beginning to tremble.

They were going to tighten around her, Faith could tell, keep her in place until Bex came upon her tongue and she wanted it. She *longed* for it.

And for the first time, Faith was beginning to realize she deserved this.

She deserved to have someone who cherished her, who thought up cute dates and incredible play scenes, who made Faith's pleasure her goal, and let Faith taste her.

Faith deserved happiness.

There was a shout above her, and Bex's fingers tightened, before suddenly going slack as she writhed beneath Faith's mouth.

"Fuck, rainbow girl. I'm coming. Faith, I'm coming!"

Her cries were so loud, especially in the echo-y shower, that Faith hoped the rooms were soundproofed.

When Bex's thighs had loosened, Faith sat back and rested her chin upon Bex's knee. "I do a good job?"

"You did a fucking *incredible* job. Holy fuck that was wild."

Faith grinned and tried not to look too smug. "You're welcome."

Bex looked down at her and mussed up her hair affectionately. "We're still going to have to get that paint off you."

"I know," said Faith. "But I don't mind too much

now." It was weird, but she really didn't. It was as if getting to see Bex at the height of pleasure, in that most vulnerable of positions, had reassured Faith of Bex's trust in her.

Bex hauled Faith up to her feet and pulled her close. They stood there for several minutes, breast to breast, Faith resting her head in the crook of Bex's neck. It felt calm.

It felt right.

Eventually, Bex kissed her forehead and sat her down. "I'll be gentle, I promise."

This time she got the peach-scented body wash from the caddy on the wall, applied it to a washcloth and carefully ran it all over Faith's back and shoulders. The touch was soothing, and when she eventually turned the shower wand's spray to Faith's body, the rainbow swirls of water didn't make her sad anymore, they made her smile. Gentle strokes alternating with the spray of water cleaned much of the paint away.

Cleaning her ass was slightly more complicated, and a lot more amusing. It couldn't happen whilst they were sitting down, and the two of them joked around, with Faith pretending to go splat on the wall, and Bex spraying her as if with a hose, and then they ended with her on her hands on knees on the bench, the cloth and spray being used that way.

It made them both laugh.

As the last swirls of paint drifted down the drain, Bex leaned down and kissed Faith. "Gods you're beautiful, rainbow girl, with or without paint."

CHAPTER Nineteen

Bex wrapped them both up in huge fluffy bath sheets and they scuttled from the bathroom to the main part of the suite. Faith flomped on the bed dramatically.

"Time for food?" Bex asked her.

She nodded enthusiastically. "Feed me!"

Grinning, Bex grabbed the phone and called down to the Italian restaurant. "Can we order mac and cheese for two please? With some of that garlic focaccia I saw on the menu yesterday?"

They assured her they absolutely could, and it'd be delivered within half an hour. That was a huge relief. After so much play, they needed refueling.

She grabbed two bottles of water from the fridge and joined Faith on the bed.

"Here you go, drink up," she said.

Faith pulled a face. "Water? Nah, I'm fine."

Bex knew her face must have been a picture because Faith's eyes widened and she took the bottle from her hurriedly, opened the lid and gulped down almost half its contents at once. She'd forgotten what effect her Domme face could have, mainly because Bex was only just realizing that she'd barely used it this weekend.

She'd topped Faith multiple times, sure, but it had felt so natural, like so much of an extension of who they were, that she hadn't had to put on the Domme persona she usually adopted in clubs.

That was curious.

"Oh, I actually feel better for drinking water."

"Of course you do," said Bex. "Now finish the rest of it. You started sub dropping before in the shower, and dehydration is one of the things that can exacerbate that. So drink up."

"You need to drink yours too," said Faith. "Top drop is a thing too."

She was right, of course, as Bex had found out the hard way when she'd been merely a baby Domme, so she drank her water too.

"What do we do now?" asked Faith.

"What would you like to do?" asked Bex back. "Food'll be here in half an hour."

"Hmmm… cuddles until then, and then we pick a film to watch after?"

"Perfect," said Bex, discarding her towel and going in for cuddles.

Faith squealed. "I didn't mean *naked* cuddles!"

"Oh, you didn't?" Bex made as if she were going to put her towel back on.

"No no no!" Faith grabbed it and threw it across the room. "Much better."

She smiled at Bex and Bex couldn't help herself, she leaned in and kissed her with all the care and devotion she could muster. It had been forty-eight hours by now. Forty-eight short hours that they'd known each other, and Bex was falling fast. She wouldn't be surprised if she were head over heels in love by the time they left Rawhide Ranch tomorrow afternoon.

Faith kissed her back.

It was a precious thing, Faith's trust. Bex got the feeling she didn't give it easily, but she'd given it eagerly over the last few days. And each time she kissed Bex, it was as if she were handing her a tiny fragile butterfly, its wings fluttering in the palm of Bex's hands.

Faith felt as delicate as Bex did, and Bex wanted to be as careful with both of their emotions as she possibly could. But it didn't stop her from giving of her own trust so completely.

Having Faith between her legs, kissing and licking and sucking had been such a complete headfuck. It had changed everything Bex had thought about being a Dominant. It wasn't about having power or being in control—although that was, of course, part of it—it was about gifting the other person with whatever experience they needed. About guiding them through difficult moments, about bringing them pleasure, about letting them be able to let go of everything that worried them and allow them to be truly in the moment.

And being able to do that for someone was in itself, a gift.

"I—" she began, and then cut off. How could she say that she loved Faith? It was something she felt, true, but to say it this early? That was ridiculous. So, she softened the sentiment. "I feel like I'm falling for you." That sounded better, more reasonable, and it had the added bonus of being true.

Faith sat up and looked at her. "That feels like a big thing to say."

Bex felt a kick of panic, but she took a breath and concentrated on keeping her breathing even, as if that would prevent her from spiraling. "I guess so, yeah."

"I feel the same way," Faith said. "Which is scary because we haven't known each other very long."

"Right?" Thank goodness Faith was having the same feelings, and the same doubts Bex was. "I'm not suggesting that we U-Haul or anything, but I don't want the end of this weekend to be the end of us."

"It won't be," said Faith with absolute certainty. "I mean, we even live in the same city. The universe is yelling at us pretty loudly; we'd be fools if we tried to ignore it."

Bex didn't know about the universe yelling at them or anything, but if she thought about it, cosmic interference might be the best way to explain how she felt like she'd been hit by a thunderbolt. Like some god of love had notched an arrow in his bow and aimed it straight at her heart.

There was a knock at the door and Faith, seemingly oblivious to the fact that she was the answer to all of Bex's hopes and dreams, bounced off the bed, grabbed a robe and opened the door.

Luckily, the bed was round the corner and out of sight, because Bex was laid out, completely bowled over by the fact that she might actually be in some kind of relationship.

Chapter Twenty

The mac and cheese was *heaven*, especially when paired with the most garlicky of garlic breads. And it was focaccia, which made everything better. Tender and crispy, it had pockets of flavor that made Faith moan with every bite.

Bex was very quiet as they ate.

Faith kept sneaking looks at her, but each time Bex caught her looking, Bex was the one to blush and duck her head. What on earth…?

"Bex, what's going on?"

"Nothing," she mumbled.

Faith put her spoon down—which was difficult because this mac and cheese was absolutely heavenly—and looked sternly at her. "*Bex*," she said, putting a significant amount of emphasis on the other woman's name. "What is going on?"

"I need a bit more of an idea about what 'this won't be the end us' means."

Faith almost laughed but didn't when she saw Bex's face. It was the most neurospicy thing that she'd ever heard a neurotypical say. "That's fair. Do you want me to explain what it means to me, or would you like to say what it means to you?"

"You, please," said Bex.

It was obvious to Faith that Bex was worrying about whether she was misinterpreting what Faith had said, because that was exactly the kind of thing that Faith tended to worry about herself.

"Well, I'd like us to date," said Faith. "I don't really know what that looks like exactly, because I'm not exactly experienced in this whole relationship thing."

Bex looked thoughtful. "Exclusively?"

Faith's stomach sank. She'd considered trying polyamory before, and she knew people for whom it worked very well, but she didn't know if she had the nervous system for it. The idea of Bex dating her and then dating someone else, made her feel small and insignificant. She'd never had someone make her their main priority, and if she were polyamorous, she'd constantly worry if that was going to happen here too. "I mean, I'd prefer to be exclusive." She tried to keep her tone light, but her emotions were churning underneath.

"Good," said Bex. "It might be selfish of me, but I don't like the idea of you with anyone else."

The sigh of relief Faith let out was loud. Bex looked up at her and laughed. "Oh shit, you were worried about it too? We're a bit of a pair, aren't we?"

"Just a little bit," said Faith. "Okay, so why don't we say that we're dating? And the rest of it will all fall into place in time, I'm sure."

"That sounds good," said Bex, and smiled shyly.

"Now can I finish eating my mac and cheese?" Faith knew she sounded slightly grumpy, but mac and cheese!

"Absolutely," said Bex.

The film they picked out was one with lots of explosions, something beyond silly, and the perfect end to the perfect day. They curled up on the couch together, not bothering with clothes, and covered themselves with a big blanket.

This time it was Faith who fell asleep first, drifting off, curled up against Bex, and snoring intermittently, from the way she jerked awake every now and then.

Bex looked beyond amused by the whole situation.

"Are you literally snoring yourself awake?" she asked and Faith had merely stuck her tongue out and commented that Bex should invest in a pair of very good earplugs.

They tumbled into bed together, fairly early, and were both conked out within minutes. No time for sexiness or making out because they'd managed to tucker themselves out completely.

Faith woke up first again, the next morning.

Bex was still asleep next to her, but instead of getting up and making breakfast again, Faith rolled over and cuddled up close. Bex mumbled something and rolled over until she was spooning Faith.

She liked how their respective roles in a scene didn't determine who was big spoon and who was little spoon. She liked both positions, she'd discovered this weekend, although this morning Bex curled up against her was doing things to Faith.

She wriggled her ass where she fit against Bex and Bex groaned sleepily and bit her shoulder.

Faith squeaked, and Bex flung an arm over her and pulled her back close. "Hush up, squeaky. Lie here and feel all silky against me."

"I'm not squeaky!" said Faith in what was, it had to be admitted, a squeaky voice.

Bex bit her neck this time, and then sucked and kissed, and Faith proved Bex's point by making a whole array of noises that ranged from high pitched to ones only dogs could hear. She felt the rumble of Bex's laugh before she heard it, and it heated her skin.

"My squeaky toy," said Bex, and rolled over until she was above Faith, nestled between her legs.

She ground up against her, and Faith was wet. Very fucking wet.

"Kiss me," she whispered, and Bex leaned down and did just that. Soft butterfly kisses that peppered her jawline and her cheeks until finally—*finally*—she reached Faith's lips.

Faith almost sighed into that kiss, melting in Bex's arms.

Bex ground against her again, making little circular motions with her hips and Faith whispered, "More."

"More? You want more, rainbow girl?"

"Yes. Right now."

Bex pressed a burning kiss to her lips and then moved up and away. Faith frowned at the sudden distance and reached up to pull her back.

"Uh uh, I'm just thinking. You know how you liked me filling you up?"

Fuck yes she'd liked being filled up.

"Well, I have my strap-on in my bag. How would you like to be filled up with that?"

Faith's eyes widened and she nodded. Yes. Yes, absolutely yes. That sounded like the perfect way to start this day.

"Okay, give me a second." Bex got tangled in the sheets and fell off the bed in her hurry to get to her bag.

"You okay?" asked Faith, sitting up and peering over the edge of the bed to see where Bex was in a heap on the floor.

Bex bounced back up and grinned. "Yup, just a minor setback!" She rushed across the room and was soon back, complete with harness, strap-on and lube.

The strap-on looked large, and Bex leaned over and kissed Faith. "Don't worry, with the way you took my fingers yesterday, this'll be a doozy. And it looks larger than it is, I promise."

Faith was going to have to take Bex's word for it. The harness looked complicated to put on, but Bex managed it and then shifted until she was over Faith once more.

"Look at me," she said, and Faith obeyed. "It's just us. It's just me."

Nodding, Faith leaned up and kissed Bex, which settled her nerves. "We've got this."

"We've got this," agreed Bex.

She didn't use the strap-on straight away, but instead returned to kissing Faith, making her way down her neck to each breast, nibbling as she went.

There were inevitably more squeaks, and that helped Faith relax, until Bex's mouth was at her pussy, and she kissed her there as well.

"*Bex!*" Somehow, it was that kiss, delivered by Bex so perfectly, that almost undid Faith. She writhed and gasped, and when Bex slipped two—no, three—fingers inside of her, she was so wet there was no resistance whatsoever.

"You're so wet for me," Bex said, her eyes dark with desire. "All for me, my lovely rainbow girl."

"Yes," said Faith. "All for you."

"Would you like…?"

"Now please," said Faith. She needed Bex as close to her as possible, bodies slick with sweat and touching, and that wasn't happening with fingers between them.

She'd lubed up the strap-on already, and so slowly inched forward, giving Faith time to adjust.

Faith felt so *full*, or at least she thought she did, until Bex withdrew and thrust back in with such precision that Faith's eyes rolled upward and her sight almost whited out.

"What the fuck?" she said, and then, when Bex paused, "don't stop! For God's sake, do *not* stop."

"I love it when you get all demanding," said Bex. "That's it, rainbow girl, tell me what you want. Tell me what you need."

"You," Faith almost growled out. "I need you."

Bex took Faith's right leg and placed it on her shoulder, and then pushed at Faith's left knee until it spread open for her. "You've got me." She paused then, looking down at Faith's pussy, filled with her strap-on. "Come on, pretty rainbow girl, beg me for it."

"Fuck you," said Faith, and grinned. "Fuck, Bex, you know I need it."

In one swift movement, Bex slammed into Faith so deep that Faith finally understood what people said about seeing stars. Bex took up a rhythm that was faster than Faith knew was possible. "You're going to come on my strap-on," Bex told her. "You're going to come apart for me, and then, once you're spent, you're going to touch my clit and I will shatter for you. My perfect rainbow girl, all wet and needy for me."

Faith was wet and needy.

And desperate.

She needed to come for Bex.

Bex leaned down so that their noses touched, never once pausing the movement of her hips. "I've got you, rainbow girl. Come for me."

CHAPTER Twenty-one

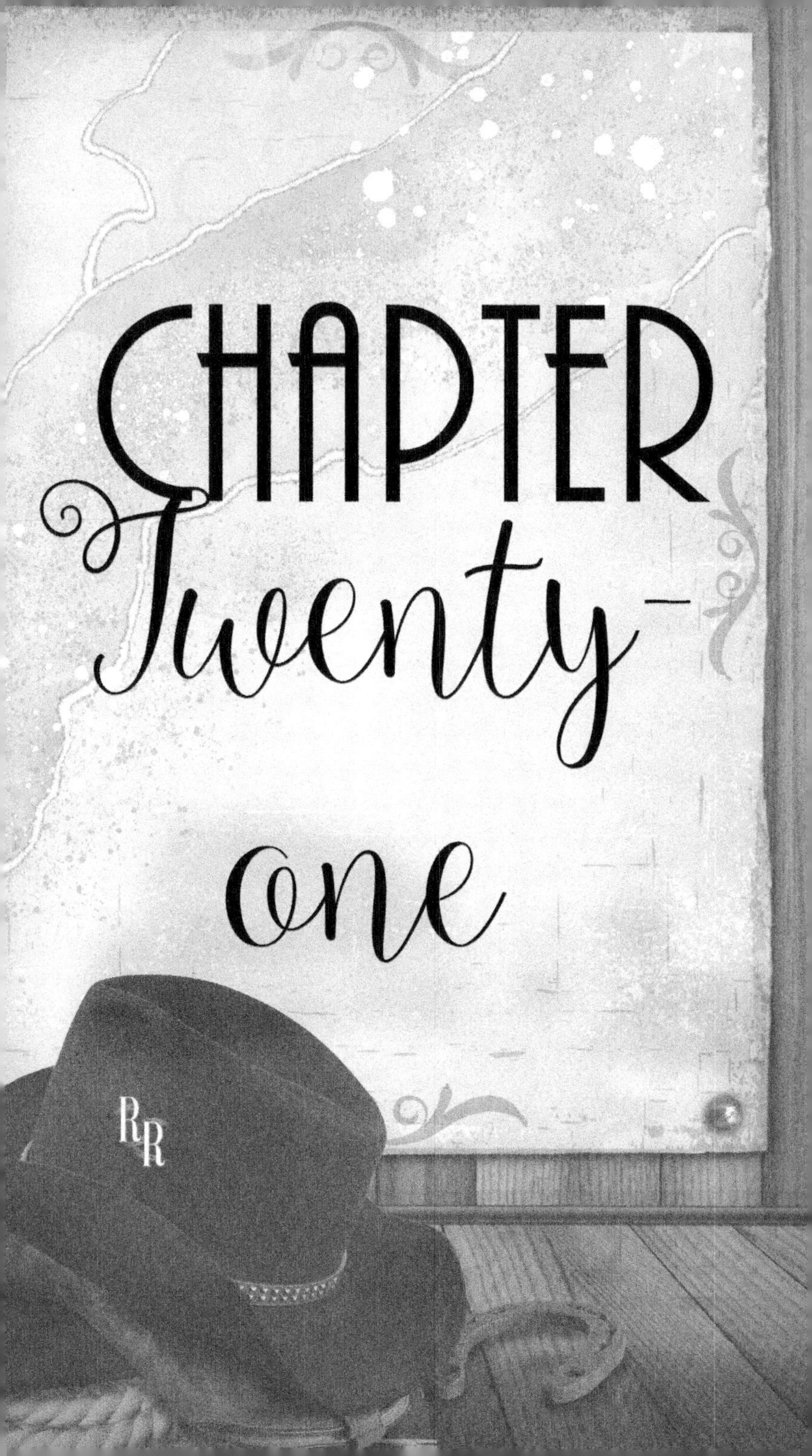

Faith's whole body shook as she came, her mouth open in a soundless cry. But her eyes never left Bex.

"That's my girl," said Bex, fiercely proud of them both. "And again."

"Again?" asked Faith, her voice hoarse.

Bex reached her hand down to brush Faith's clit and didn't ease up with her thrusts. "Again."

The look of surprise on Faith's face as her pleasure peaked a second time filled Bex with happiness. The harness she wore rubbed against her own clit in just the right way, and the feel of Faith in her arms, coming apart for her was almost too much for Bex to bear.

Faith fell back against the pillows, one hand reaching up to caress Bex's cheek. "Wow," she said simply, and then her smile turned wicked. "Your turn."

Bex hadn't been lying when she'd said to Faith that all it would take would be the touch of her hand.

Faith somehow made short work of the harness— always impressive— and then lay Bex down on her side. "Let me look at you as you come," she said, and Bex had no idea what her O-face looked like, and certainly wasn't sure about showing it to Faith, but then a thumb brushed against her clit and she was lost.

She shattered. Broke apart completely and went flying to the four corners of the universe. It was as if she were floating far outside of herself, which had her body convulse and tremble and her voice grow hoarse from screaming.

And then there was that gentle touch against her

face, the caressing of her cheek, and Faith drew Bex back down, back into her body.

She curled up and buried her face in Faith's shoulder and hung on as if her life depended on it.

"I've got you," said Faith, echoing her own words back at her. "It's okay, Bex, I've got you."

"I know you have," muttered Bex against her skin. In this moment, she would have trusted Faith with everything—even her life. She'd never felt so safe in a lover's arms.

When she could move again, Bex rolled over onto her back and stared up at the ceiling. "Well, fuck," she said.

"Exactly," said Faith. "Water?"

Bex nodded and padded across the room to the kitchenette to get them both a bottle each. She tossed one to Faith who caught it neatly, and then took a long drink from her own.

"I'm going to make breakfast," she announced. "It's not going to be nearly as fancy as your pancakes yesterday, but I can definitely manage marmalade on toast without fucking it up."

"That sounds great," said Faith. "I might jump in the shower while you do that?"

"Go for it," said Bex, and leaned down to kiss her rainbow girl before wandering over to the kitchenette.

Toast was pretty simple, and she'd brought a jar of marmalade with her for the weekend. There was nothing quite like the homemade marmalade Wendy made, and she and Riley had sent some jars over, along with other British treats, when Bex had first moved. It was rich and warming, with just a touch of whisky running through it.

The toast was all buttered and she was just applying the marmalade as Faith came out of the shower, a towel turbaned up around her head. She'd left the rest of herself bare.

"You look almost as delicious as the toast," joked Bex.

Faith declared the marmalade delicious and devoured her toast pretty quickly. Bex ate slower, savoring the taste.

"I promised Mandi I'd have lunch with her, and that I'd spend the morning with her too, if you don't mind?"

"Of course not," said Bex. "I completely understand. What time are you heading off today?"

"The cab is picking me up around two to take me to Porter's Corner," said Faith. "Then I'll catch the bus back to Billings."

Bex frowned. "Well, I'm driving back, so if you're comfortable with it, I could drive you home. You shouldn't have to spend all that money on a taxi and bus if you don't have to."

"That… that would be nice." Faith blushed. "And we'll see if we can stand each other after being stuck in a car together for over four hours."

Bex laughed. "Oh, you're definitely going to regret that when you hear my singing." She grinned. "Gotta sing whilst driving."

"It's a plan," said Faith.

Even so, Bex felt the loss of her when Faith left to go meet Mandi, and she realized that part of the reason she'd come here in the first place was to try and make some friends. To build a new kinky community for herself, and she still wanted that.

Getting dressed, she wandered down to the lobby, and almost bumped into Drake.

"Hey," she said.

"Morning," he said. "I see you managed to get all the paint off."

That made her laugh. "It took a lot of body wash," she admitted, "and a very long shower."

"Sounds terrible," he said, and grinned.

"Are you working security now?" she asked, "Only asking as I've got time to kill, and I've been so wrapped up in Faith that I haven't actually had the chance to make many friends."

"Sure," he said. "Luna should be off duty as well; we can all grab a coffee together if you like?"

The three of them got takeaway cups from the café and went to go sit on the porch that spread across the front of the main building.

"This is the first time I've actually seen a lodge like this," said Bex. "They always look so idyllic, but the UK's pretty small so there's rarely enough room for buildings like this. Especially in cities. Your state is fifty-five percent bigger than our entire country, so it stands to reason you have more space."

"It's cozy," said Luna. "And the Ranch is always peaceful this time on a Sunday. The Littles aren't wreaking havoc just yet, and it's a Sunday so a lot of the ranch hands get to sleep in slightly later than usual. How've you found your stay?"

"Great," said Bex. "Though it feels like a weekend isn't nearly long enough. I imagine that Faith and I will be coming back to visit again pretty soon."

"Together?" asked Drake, the large man leaning back on a swing seat.

"I hope so," said Bex. "We're going to try dating." She paused and then added in a flurry, "I'm crazy about her and I don't understand how. It's not even been three days and I'd do anything for the woman."

Luna reached out and squeezed her hand.

"And it's not even like it's just a dynamic thing. *She* holds *me* in her arms. She big spoons me! *I'm* the big spoon."

"I'm glad," said Luna. "It sounds like she's really good for you. Sometimes we forget that Tops need looking after too."

She looked at Drake then, who was swinging on the swing, and didn't appear to notice. Bex looked down and hid a smile. "I guess so. It's just different from anything I've had before, and it's thrown me a bit."

Drake stopped his swinging and looked at Bex. "Do you care about her?"

"Yes." There wasn't even the slightest hesitation in Bex's response.

"Then you'll be able to work it out. Just talk to each other, and keep having fun, and see where it goes. That's all you can do sometimes."

CHAPTER Twenty-two

Faith and Mandi were having lunch in the Italian restaurant. "Tay's got the day off, and wanted to join us," Mandi said. "Is that okay with you? I know you said you were keen to make more friends."

Faith nodded. Tay had been a whirlwind of fun when she'd met them on Friday, and they'd clicked instantly.

They came and joined them when Faith and Mandi sat down, flouncing in wearing a leather vest and a floral skirt. "What do you think?" they asked, twirling on the spot.

Mandi rolled her eyes and waved at them to sit down, but Faith grinned. "It looks great; a fantastic blend of two different fabrics."

"Of course, you're an artist, aren't you? Well, if you say it looks good, and you have an eye for art, then that practically makes me a fashionista!" They clambered onto one of the chairs, and sat, half on, half off.

"ADHDers," said Mandi, with a giggle.

Tay stuck their tongue out at her. "The 'tism speaks!"

Faith giggled at the two of them. They both appeared to be in some kind of Middle headspace, not quite Little, but not quite Big.

"Speaking of art," said Mandi, "how did you like the paints I popped into the picnic basket for you? I managed to get Amelia to sneak them over to Tay for you."

"The paints were great—as was the picnic, by the way," said Faith. "So delicious."

"I am very good at picnics," agreed Tay. "Chef

Guilia lets me deal with all of the ones ordered from our kitchen. It makes a change from pasta."

"Yes yes," said Mandi, waving her hand at Tay. "You're a culinary genius, we know. Did you get to use the paints?"

Faith flushed a deep red and the two Littles looked at her curiously.

"Does painting usually evoke that response in people?" asked Tay out the corner of their mouth to Mandi, deliberately hamming it up.

Mandi giggled. "Definitely not, I think Faith might be hiding something from us."

"I mean, I am," said Faith. "But I can't talk to you guys about it if you're in Middle-space. That'd be too weird."

There was an imperceptible shift, and Mandi and Tay nodded. "We can be Big," said Mandi, smiling. "Remember where we met?"

"Definitely," agreed Tay.

"Okay then. Well, Bex came up with an idea for a scene, using the paint." She paused and looked at them. "Are you sure…?"

"Just get on with it!" said Tay impatiently.

"Tay!" said Mandi. "It might be private."

"I want to tell you, it's just it's quite…" Faith's voice trailed off, and she smiled in remembrance.

"That's a happy face if ever I saw one," said Tay, grabbing a piece of garlic bread and taking a bite.

"You have no idea," said Faith, shifting on her chair and leaning forward. "Okay, so she found this branch—from an aspen, because they have these heart-shaped leaves—and then she organized for them to cover one of the private playrooms in plastic sheets, and then she used the branch as a flogger."

"How do the paints come into it, though?" asked Mandi.

Faith blushed. "We covered the branch and leaves in paint, and she used my back as a canvas."

Both Tay and Mandi looked at her, open mouthed.

"I did say it was something for Bigs."

They rushed to reassure her.

"I mean, it sounds like it'd be sensory hell for me," said Mandi, shuddering. "The branch might be okay, but the paint? Absolutely not."

Tay looked thoughtful. "I don't think I'd want paint, but you could do something similar with food. Maybe with ice cream!"

Mandi looked at her. "Chef Guilia's ice cream?"

"You never know," said Tay, pulling a face at her friend. "But yeah, what an amazing idea! You literally became the art."

"Right?" said Faith. "And Bex calls me rainbow girl now, which is just…" She smiled and sighed happily. "Just the best."

"It's a shame photos aren't allowed," said Tay. "Because I bet that looked *incredible*."

"We got official permission," said Faith. "Bex was allowed to take some photos, but only on my phone, and with no indication of where we were. It's just of my back, really—she cut the bulk of my bum out of the pictures—so would you guys like to see?"

"*Would* we?" asked Tay. "I mean, I certainly would!"

"It's just your back?" asked Mandi. "Because I don't know how comfortable I'd be seeing someone other than my Amelia naked from the front."

"It's all from the back," Faith reassured her.

"Then it's fine," said Mandi. "And I'm glad because I want to see!"

Faith dug her phone out of her pocket and selected her favorite of the photos. The two of them poured over it, making it larger and exclaiming at the patterns.

"There's such a great contrast with the lines of paint from the twigs, and the pretty heart and half-heart shapes from the leaves," said Mandi. "And this photo looks seriously good—you look like you belong in an art gallery."

"I do belong in an art gallery," said Faith. "It's just that I've never been the art myself before. I'm used to making the art."

"I get that," said Tay. "I'm great at cooking, but food play in a kink scene is a completely different vibe altogether."

Faith and Mandi stared at them.

"What?" they asked defensively. "I'm not always in Little space, and I had a thriving sex life before I came to Rawhide." They muttered something else about ice cream under their voice that Faith didn't quite catch, but Chef Guilia made homemade ice cream, and she guessed the chef might explain somewhat why Tay had food play on the brain. "Anyway, back to you, and how ridiculously cute you and Bex are."

Mandi reached over and held Faith's hand. "You really like her, don't you?"

"Yes. I just don't know how she does it. She sees me, all of me." She looked at Mandi. "When we first met, I was sad because I was lonely, and I felt completely unseen. You and Amelia saw me and took me out for food and somehow became my friends. Without you both, I'd never have gotten here. But that was the first time I ever felt like someone saw me. And now?" Her eyes filled with tears. "Now I have Bex."

"Have you told her this?" asked Tay, unusually quiet.

"Because sometimes, if you wait too long to tell someone how you feel about them, it can be too late."

"I don't think it's ever too late," said Mandi, but Tay shrugged her comment off.

"I still think you should say something."

"I have, and she has too. It's scary, feeling this intensely so quickly, but we're going to date. She's offered to drive me home today, instead of me having to take a cab and bus, and I've taken her up on that. It'll be nice to hang out with her in a completely neutral setting—not a dungeon, or a bedroom, or on a picnic blanket by a lake."

"Yeah," said Mandi. "It's how someone is in the everyday that I like the most." She grinned at Tay. "Like how you're always chaotic, but always kind. And how Amelia's firmness is rooted in love. It's made me come out of my shell more."

"Yes," agreed Tay. "You were absolutely terrified of your own shadow when you first arrived. And look at you now, making new friends, sassing me… Even Ralphie says that you look happier."

"I am," she said. "And I just know, Faith, that Bex is going to be the same for you. I just know it."

CHAPTER Twenty-three

There was a whole cavalcade of people who came to see them both off. Bex felt slightly overwhelmed by it all. Even despite the fact that Bex and Faith had spent most of their time together, the people they'd come into contact with had all come out to say their goodbyes.

Mandi, Amelia and Tay stood with a woman in chef's whites who Bex assumed was Chef Guilia. Tay had another picnic hamper for them—"To stop off on the drive home," they said—and Chef Guilia handed over a small coolbox that Bex could plug into her car.

"Some ice cream," she said. "Rainbow colored."

Faith flushed at that as Tay waggled their eyebrows behind Chef Guilia's back.

The older woman didn't even turn around. "Tay, stop that."

"Yes, Chef," said Tay cheerfully, and then they added, "I only told her that Bex calls you rainbow girl, promise."

From Faith's sigh of relief, Bex had guessed that she'd told Tay and Mandi all about their art scene. She didn't mind. She wanted the whole world to know what beautiful art her rainbow girl made.

Luna and Drake had come over as well, and even Derek Hawkins came out of his office to say goodbye. When Luna hugged Bex, she whispered in her ear. "Remember what I said, Tops deserve to feel looked after too. You deserve this happiness."

Bex was too overcome to do anything but squeeze Luna tight, and smile at her when she let go.

Derek strode over and shook hands with them both. "You've had a good stay?"

They both nodded.

"It's been excellent," said Faith. "Truly. And we'll be back to visit, won't we, Bex?"

All heads swung in her direction, and Bex fought the urge to take a step back. "Yes," she said. "For a week, next time. And perhaps, if we're allowed, during some of the holidays—I imagine parties here are an absolute hoot."

"They are," said Mandi. She and Amelia stepped forward to hug Faith.

Her rainbow girl looked close to tears. "Thank you," she said. "For everything. I can't believe how much meeting the two of you has changed my life."

"You've changed your own life," said Amelia. "You were the one who was brave enough to come, all on your own. Look at what that small step has produced." The tall woman hugged Faith. "Come back and visit us any time, and maybe we'll come visit you in the city too."

"Please do," said Faith. "We'd love that."

She slipped her hand into Bex's and Bex couldn't have felt prouder. "Yes," she agreed. "You all should come visit us, any time you like."

They got into Bex's car, and strapped in, set off for Billings.

"It's a four hour drive," warned Bex.

Faith looked nonplussed. "I know, not far at all."

That made Bex laugh. "I forget how you Americans are about travel sometimes," she said. "A four-hour drive in the UK is considered a fairly lengthy thing. It's actually illegal to drive for more than six hours without having a break."

"Well," said Faith. "I don't think we consider

anything really long unless its five hours or more. Some people drive twelve hours before taking a break which seems like a doozy to me." She paused. "Are you going to be okay driving for four hours? Although I guess it would be longer if we take a break for our picnic."

"Oh, I'll be fine," said Bex. "Just checking on you." She looked over at her rainbow girl as they waited for the iron gates at the end of the driveway to open. "How about we drive straight home, and then have the picnic at mine? Or at yours, if you prefer."

Faith's smile back was sunny. "How are you so good at coming up with these ideas? That sounds lovely. If we go to yours, it means you can park and then just crash once we're done with the picnic. Why don't we do that?"

She was so sweet and thoughtful. "Fine, but I'm paying for your cab home after, if you don't stay." Bex fixed her gaze on the road and tried to ignore the cheeky grin that spread across Faith's face.

"You'd like me to stay?"

"You know I would, rainbow girl, but I also understand if you're all peopled out after this weekend, and just want to sleep in your own bed."

"I mean, sure I'm peopled out," said Faith, "but you don't count as people."

Well, wasn't that the most adorable thing for her to say. Made Bex feel all soft and warm. "I don't think I've ever been more glad not to count as people," she said.

"Good," said Faith. "Because it's the biggest compliment I can give someone. Now, you said something about bad singing?"

Bex got Faith to open Spotify on her own phone, and search for Bex's favorite driving playlists. They plumped for one filled with 80s rock music, and Bex was delighted to note that Faith knew the words to every single one.

She also had a significantly better singing voice than Bex, and it would probably have been more tuneful if Bex had quietened down and let her lead the singing.

Bex was not that kind of singer. She was passionate, she was loud and she was out of tune.

Faith didn't care though. Bex had accepted her, just as she was, and she was determined to do the same—and if that meant enthusiastically embracing singing at the top of her voice, so be it. The two of them sung their hearts out all the way to Billings.

CHAPTER Twenty-four

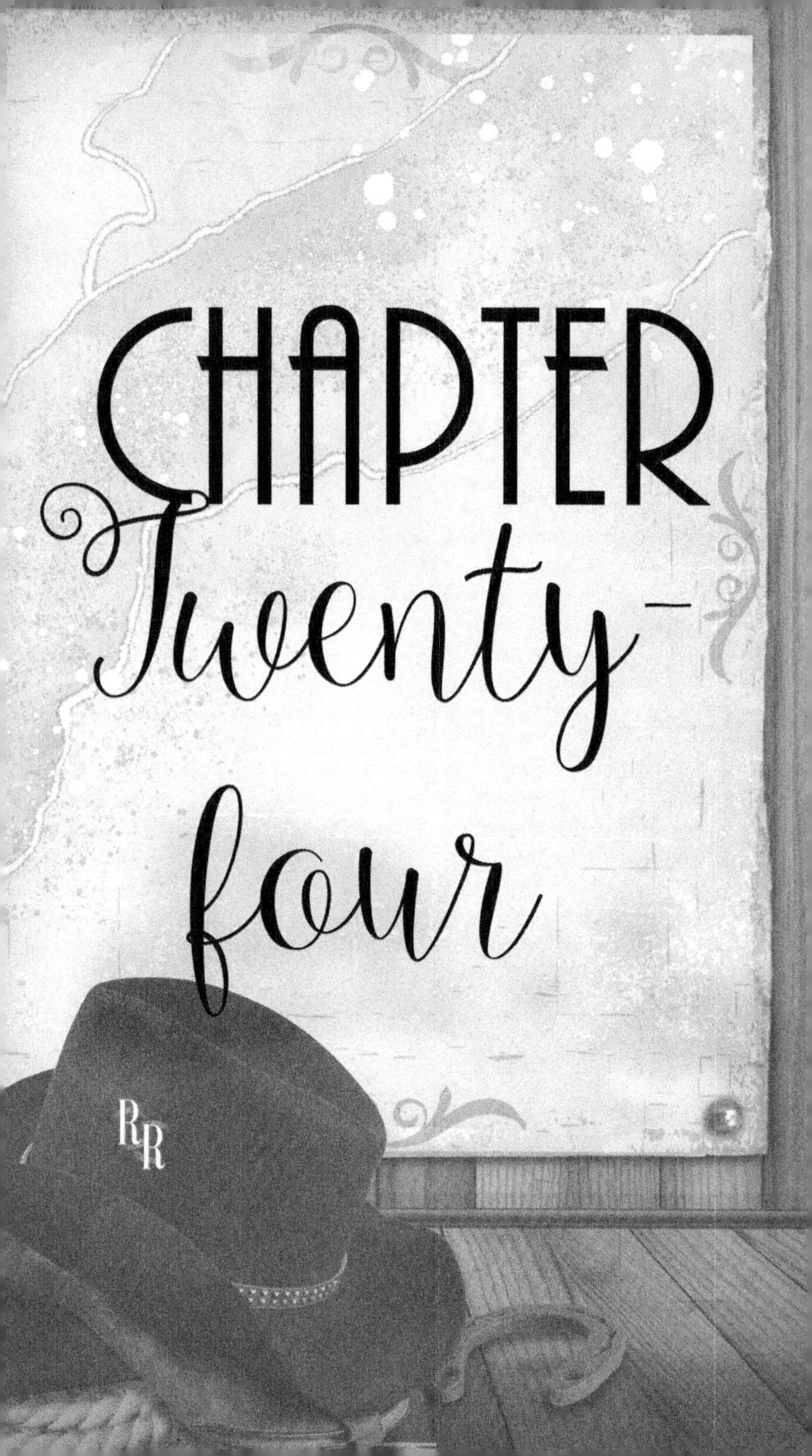

After Bex had parked, they took the elevator up to her apartment. The elevator kept going up and up and up, and Faith looked at Bex suspiciously.

"Where exactly do you live?" she asked.

Bex mumbled something about having the top floor and Faith stared at her.

"A penthouse? You live in a penthouse?!"

"No, not a penthouse. But, well, a really lovely loft." When Faith kept staring, Bex clarified. "Look, the consultancy firm I work for *really* wanted me to move out here and set up a new branch because they liked what I did in the UK. And I held out long enough for them to find me an incredible apartment to rent at cost."

"I bet at cost is still really expensive," said Faith. "Bet it's more than a potter could afford." She was joking, but there was a kernel of truth in her words. Back at Rawhide Ranch, they'd been the same, equal, and she'd forgotten that out here, in the real world, that wasn't quite how things worked.

Bex pulled a face. "I mean, it's still pretty pricey, but I go into businesses and boss them around until they do what I say and then make a massive profit. They can afford to pay me pretty well. But I can't do what you do—create something out of nothing. And then there's all that outreach work you do. You make a big impact on the world, rainbow girl."

"Do you like your job?" Faith asked.

"Sometimes," said Bex. "Sometimes I just want to yeet, um, throw them all out a window. But the firm has said I can take on one pro bono client a year, so it's worth it, just for that. It's not working with trans and enby kids one on one, but I help make sure the charities and programs that work with them are as efficient as they can be."

Faith smiled. "Why is it that your English sounds so much more fun than my English? I'm definitely going to be stealing some of your slang even if you threaten to *yeet* me out the window," she teased before slipping her hand into the crook of Bex's arm. "As far as our contributions, don't belittle what you do as being less important than what I do. We all do what we can."

But when the elevator doors opened onto Bex's loft, she stood there, slack-jawed for a moment or two.

"*This* is your apartment. This." When you walked to the windows, you could see out across the entire city to the mountains beyond. "Oh. That's stunning."

Bex had hurried in and was sweeping paperwork into haphazard piles when she heard Faith. "Yeah, the view's pretty good."

"Pretty good?" Faith was flabbergasted. "Stop tidying up for a moment and come and have a look."

The city stretched out beneath them both, and Faith got a glimpse of her city from the sky. She'd never seen it laid out like that before, and it made her smile.

Her fingers itched and tapped on the window.

"You want to make art." It wasn't a question.

"Yes." Gods, the art she could make in this space. She longed for her potter's wheel, to turn it and keep turning. She grinned at Bex sheepishly. "You've got a nice place."

Bex grinned back. "It'll do. Come on, I'll lay out some blankets and we can picnic on the carpet."

Tay had done a great job once more, and Chef Guilia's ice cream was a delicious way to end their picnic adventure.

Leaning back against the couch behind them, Faith sighed. "I don't remember the last time I had a weekend this good."

Bex was nestled up next to her, all soft curves pressed against Faith. "Me neither."

Looking down at Bex, she was filled with a warmth. "This is good," she said. "So good that I want to say I'm falling for you too. Falling, fallen, I don't know. All I know is that time with you makes me happy."

Bex reached up and pulled Faith down to kiss her. "You're my perfect rainbow girl. You'll stay tonight?"

"I'll stay," said Faith, and kissed her again.

EPILOGUE

TWO MONTHS LATER

It might have been Bex's birthday, but Faith was just as excited—if not more so.

"I don't want anything big," Bex had insisted, but Faith had organized a small group of people to come help them celebrate at the loft. It was made up of some of the Rawhide friends they'd made—Mandi, Amelia, Tay and Chef Guilia—but somehow, she'd managed to sneakily liaise with Riley too.

It would have been impossible to hide the fact there was a party going on, considering it was being held in Bex's loft, but Riley and Wendy flying over from the UK was one surprise Faith had determined would *not* be ruined.

"What're we doing again?" asked Bex, coming from the bedroom into the open plan loft space. She was wearing a suit, the jacket unbuttoned, and her shirt open at the top. Faith still wasn't entirely sure how Bex managed to contain her curves within the shirt, and considering how some of the buttons were straining, she thought there might be a mini fashion emergency later.

Or rather, she *hoped* that there'd be a mini fashion emergency later.

"A dinner party seemed too formal," said Faith, "and as Chef Guilia's coming, I didn't want my cooking to be placed under her scrutiny. So it's drinks—we've got cocktails, mocktails, and beers—nibbles, and boardgames."

She'd managed to get her hands on a copy of *Rapidough*, which she thought would have the whole group in hysterics, and *Unstable Unicorns*, which she thought would entertain the Littles.

"Sounds amazing, love," said Bex. "You really do spoil me."

Faith wasn't quite so sure about that. Ever since they'd gotten back from Rawhide Ranch, she and Bex had been almost inseparable, to the point where Bex had cleared out a bedside table and a couple of drawers of her dresser for Faith to keep her things in.

If anything, Bex was the one spoiling Faith.

"Faith?"

Faith spun on the spot, and saw where Bex was frozen, staring at the table. "What? What's the matter?"

"Where on earth did you…? How did you…? Faith," Bex said finally. Maybe she'd finish a sentence this time. "Faith, you can't get most of this food over here. Is that Ribena? *Did you get me Ribena*?"

Faith sent a silent prayer of thanks towards Riley and Wendy, who'd shipped goodness only knows how many British goodies and treats to Faith's work over the last month.

"I mean, I had some help, but yes."

Bex came around the table and caught Faith up in her arms. "You, rainbow girl, are the best girlfriend *ever*! What would I do without you?"

"I'm not sure you want me to answer that," said Faith, who truly wasn't.

"Neither do I," said Bex, and kissed her.

Kissing Bex never got old. In fact, Faith was convinced it got better every time their lips met. She leaned into her girlfriend and savored the moment. The quiet before the storm.

Eventually though, she had to pull away. "People will be here soon," she said, and right on cue, the elevator dinged.

"Happy birthday!" chorused the group they found

inside. And then Mandi and Tay were bounding through, followed by Amelia holding a pile of presents and Chef Guilia with what looked like a birthday cake.

Bex hugged each of them, and her mouth dropped open when she saw the traditional Italian birthday cake Chef Guilia had made. "That looks *incredible*!" she said.

"The rest of the food is less exciting," said Faith, pointing towards the beige spread that had sent Bex into raptures. "But I have it on good authority that it's yummy."

"You'd better believe it!" said Bex. "There're stuffed Yorkshires, Amelia."

Amelia looked a little nonplussed. "Isn't Yorkshire a place? How can you stuff it?"

Bex slung her arm around the older woman's shoulder and walked her over to the spread, talking about savory pancakes and roast beef fillings.

"I put here?" asked Chef Guilia, and quietly went and set up the cake.

"Everything still in place for the big arrival?" asked Tay.

Faith nodded. "And I don't think she suspects a thing, either."

"Brilliant," said Tay. "Wow, this is exciting. Surprises are so much better when you know you're not going to get punished for them after."

"Those aren't surprises though, Tay," pointed out Mandi. "Those are pranks."

"Oh yeah," said Tay, and they grinned mischievously. "Pranks."

The sound of a phone cut through the hum of conversation, and Bex grabbed hers from her back pocket and apologized to everyone. "So sorry, it's my best friend, she's in the UK. Hey, Riley!" she said, answering the call. "Faith surprised me with a… wait a second. Is that…?"

She fell into silence and ran towards the elevator. There was a ding and the doors opened slowly to reveal two women, holding hands, and beaming at Bex.

"You fucking arsehole," said Bex as she threw her arms around Riley and burst into tears.

"It's okay," said Riley, patting her friend calmly on the back. "She gets a bit emosh when people are nice to her. That's why it's important to have good friends, isn't it, Bex?" she added. "So that you get used to it." Riley seemed as nice in person as she did over the phone, and Bex was clearly delighted to see her. Riley's partner, Wendy, was an older lady, with white hair and a trim figure.

"Hello," she said quietly. "It's lovely to finally meet you, Faith. I'm Wendy."

"Hi, Wendy," she replied. "Shall we leave the two of them to it for a bit?"

"That might be a good idea," the older woman agreed, and came over to meet the Rawhide Ranch crowd.

As Faith made the introductions, she kept an eye on where Bex and Riley stood, reunited. She was so pleased the plan had come off so well, but there was a small part of her that feared that seeing Riley would highlight to Bex quite how much she missed home. Faith wanted her girlfriend to be happy, more than anything, but she also wanted her here, in Billings.

Faith's routine, her schedule, helped her regulate. She didn't think that she could face moving to another country, even to be with Bex.

When the two of them came over, Bex gave her a big smacker of a kiss. "I can't believe you managed to plan all of this behind my back," she exclaimed. "You're a sneaky one, rainbow girl. I guess I'll have to keep an eye on you."

Riley hugged her too, and as everyone else went to raid the food that had been laid out, came and sat next to Faith on the couch.

"She's happy, you know?" Riley said, after a long pause. "After her dad died, and all that bullshit with her family, I don't know, it just felt like she was never going to be happy again."

Faith looked at the other woman, who smiled sadly. "You don't sound happy about it."

"I am," said Riley, "truly I am. I'm just a little sad that her life is here now, so far away. That's not"—she added hurriedly, seeing the look on Faith's face—"my way of saying her life shouldn't be here, or that she should move back home. She shouldn't, I know that. It's just hard because she is my best friend, and she's so far away."

"Well, you're welcome to visit whenever you like. And Bex has enough airmiles with her job she should be able to fly back and see you more often."

"If we can persuade her to take time off, that is," said Riley.

Faith agreed. "We'll work on her together," she said. "Maybe for Christmas?"

"Christmas would be *perfect*," said Riley. "Thank you, and thank you for looking after her. She's shining from the inside out, and I've never seen her like that before."

The boardgames were an undeniable success.

Even after fifteen years of teaching pottery to children, Faith had never seen such ridiculous sculptures. It was hysterical, although one particular rose had lips that bore a remarkable resemblance to labia. Faith was tempted to take it to work to replicate and cast it.

Finally, Bex stood to make a speech. It was short, and brief, and very much to the point. "Thank you for coming," she said. "There have been some sneaky plans concocted, for which I'm very grateful, and I am very glad to have you all in my life." She looked straight at Faith. "Especially you, rainbow girl. Thank you for a wonderful day."

"You're welcome," said Faith.

When everyone left—Mandi, Amelia, Tay and Chef Guilia for Rawhide Ranch, and Riley and Wendy to their hotel to sleep off their jetlag—and Faith and Bex were left alone, Faith decided it was now the perfect time to give Bex her present.

The best thing about working where she did was that there were artists everywhere. One of her colleagues had agreed to take the photo of their rainbow flogging session and get it printed on glass.

When light shone through it, it looked like the paint on Faith's skin was glowing.

She'd wrapped it carefully, and handed the parcel to Bex now.

"What's this?"

"Your birthday present," she said.

"But you organized all of this," Bex said. "That's more than enough birthday present, rainbow girl."

"I can take it back," said Faith, but Bex had taken it out of her hands already.

"I don't think so."

The sound of ripping paper filled the loft, and then a sharp inbreath. "Fuck, rainbow girl, it's beautiful."

The colors on the glass shone and appeared to

almost ripple as Bex moved it back and forth, getting a good look at it.

Faith flushed. "They've done a really good job, that's for sure."

Bex leaned across and bit Faith's lower lip, tugging it into her mouth and deepening the hold until Faith squeaked. "Exactly. Say thank you for the compliment."

"Thank you for the compliment." Faith couldn't resist, and hurriedly corrected it when Bex looked at her. "I'm joking, I'm joking! Thank you, Bex."

"It'll look great against the window in our bedroom. Come on, rainbow girl, I want to see if it paints your body with colored light when I put it up."

Well, that was certainly an invitation Faith wasn't going to pass up. She got up and followed Bex, only stopping when Bex paused in the doorway.

Her girlfriend looked at her with eyes that shone with desire and love. "Thank you, rainbow girl. Making my home with you feels right."

There was an answering feeling in her body that Faith couldn't ignore. "I love you."

"I love you too." Bex strode into the bedroom and Faith followed her again. The main window was to the side of the bed, and light shone across the coverlet and pillows. Bex grinned wickedly, and carefully leaned the colored glass against it.

The bed was suddenly awash with color.

"Come on, get your arse up onto this bed."

Bouncing up onto the mattress, Faith presented her arse and grinned as Bex pulled down her jeans and underwear with next to no ceremony.

She ran a finger between Faith's pussy lips and it came back wet.

"You're wet, rainbow girl. Why's that?"

"Because I want you," she said.

"I want you too," said Bex, and nudged Faith's knees apart. But instead of fingers notching themselves inside, Bex slipped between her legs and smiled up at her. The colors from the glass danced across her face, and made Faith wonder how her pussy had looked, exposed and covered in the rainbow from their flogging session. All of a sudden, she felt like art once more.

"How does it feel, being on top?" Bex asked.

"Heady," said Faith, feeling the intensity of a subspace rush over her, even in an instant.

"Good," said Bex, and then tugged on the back of Faith's thighs until she sat on Bex's face.

Her mouth was warm, her tongue teasing against Faith's clit and she gasped. "But..."

"You want me to eat your butt too?" teased Bex, and laughed at how flustered Faith got. "Come on, rainbow girl, I wanna taste you so damn bad. Treat me, it is my birthday after all."

"Fuck," said Faith as Bex hummed in approval as she started to ride her face. Her legs trembled and she had to use a hand to brace herself against the wall, in case she accidentally fell and smothered the other woman.

Her orgasm broke over her so quickly it almost felt painful, cresting with an intensity that made her shout out suddenly.

Bex carefully lifted her up, and Faith fell to the side and looked at her girlfriend next to her through eyes still clouded by desire.

"You okay there?" Bex's British accent was tinged with amusement.

Faith nodded. "Yup. Words gone."

"Your words are all gone? Well, isn't that the most adorable damn thing that I've ever heard." Bex rolled over, and straddled her waist. Slowly, she took off her blazer, and then popped each button on her shirt until her breasts fell into view, heavy and pendulous.

Shrugging her blouse off, she leaned forward until one nipple kissed Faith's lips. Faith opened her mouth and sucked it in.

"That's right, rainbow girl. Just like that."

Bex didn't even undo her pants, just ground herself against Faith's pubic bone, and then sliding down to grind on her thigh. "Fuck, rainbow girl, you feel so fucking good."

"Use me," whispered Faith, locking eyes with her. "Use me to get off, Bex."

Bex groaned then, fisting her fingers in Faith's hair and moving fast, grinding harder and harder until she came with a shout that echoed the one Faith had cried out.

She fell forward, pants still on, and rested her brow against Faith's collarbone. "Fuck, rainbow girl, that was…"

"Yeah," said Faith. "That was pretty freaking awesome." She considered continuing to lie there, the silence between them comfortable. Comforting.

But she had one final surprise.

"Hey," she said, jumping up, and then sitting heavily back down on the bed. "Got up too quickly," Faith said.

"Oh, rainbow girl," said Bex. "Come on, let's get you some water."

Faith padded after Bex back into the main room of the loft, Faith pantless, and Bex topless. They made a pair, the two of them.

Bex poured out a glass of water and stood over Faith to make sure she drank it.

"I can look after myself," protested Faith, but Bex's arched eyebrow implied otherwise.

"What was so urgent that you had to jump out from our bed anyway?" asked Bex.

"I had an idea," said Faith. "Just a small one. One last surprise."

"Go on then," said Bex.

"I'd like to make you feel like art," she said. "Not by flogging you—I think we both know that isn't really my forte—but by photographing you."

"Where?" asked Bex. She didn't seem enthusiastic, but she wasn't shutting down the idea either.

"Here," said Faith. "Here in our—your—home."

"Our home," said Bex. "You want it to be *our* home?"

This wasn't at all where Faith had envisioned this conversation going, and she really wasn't entirely certain what to make of it. She'd planned on talking about sexy photos against the window, the setting sun in the background. And by her calculations, she didn't have much time to capture it.

"Faith?"

"Yes, of course I do," she blurted out. "Of course I want to stay here with you and never leave. You're amazing. Who wouldn't want to? But right now I need you to get undressed and stand by the window so that I can take the perfect photo."

Bex didn't argue, didn't push her point, just stepped out of her pants and walked toward the window. "Where do you want me?"

Faith scampered over and shifted Bex's position so that she was looking out across the city. "There, just like that." She leaned forward and pressed a kiss to Bex's shoulder, felt the other woman shiver, and then stepped back.

The sun was just starting to set and the sky was magnificent. The colors painted Bex's skin, just like she'd painted Faith's, and the parallels took Faith's breath away.

She got out her phone and started snapping, adjusting angles, moving to capture the scene.

And then Bex looked back over her shoulder, right down the camera lens, right at Faith.

"*We're* home," she said. Not Bex, not Faith, but the both of them. Faith's heart lurched in her chest and her eyes filled with traitorous tears.

Here and now, the two of them. They were home.

"Yes," she said. "You're my home."

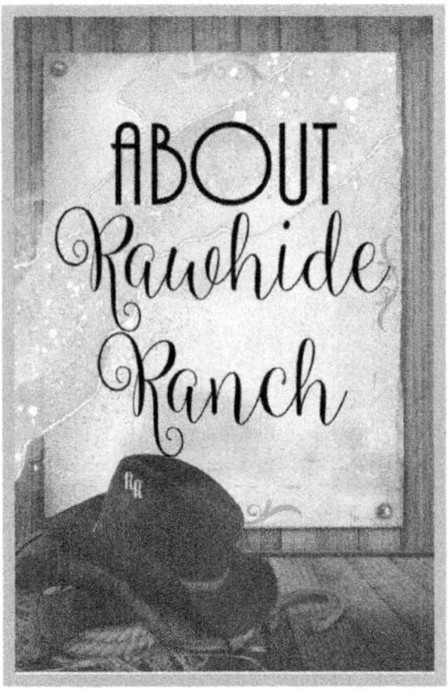

Looking for more Rawhide Ranch?

Rawhide Website: www.rawhideranchseries.com
Rawhide Ranch Newsletter: https://authoral
liebelle.eo.page/rawhideranch
Hangout & Reader Group:
https://www.facebook.com/groups/rawhideranchseries

facebook.com/RawhideRanchSeries
instagram.com/rawhideranchseries
amazon.com/Rawhide-Authors/author/B08Z8F7TPK
tiktok.com/@rawhideranchseries

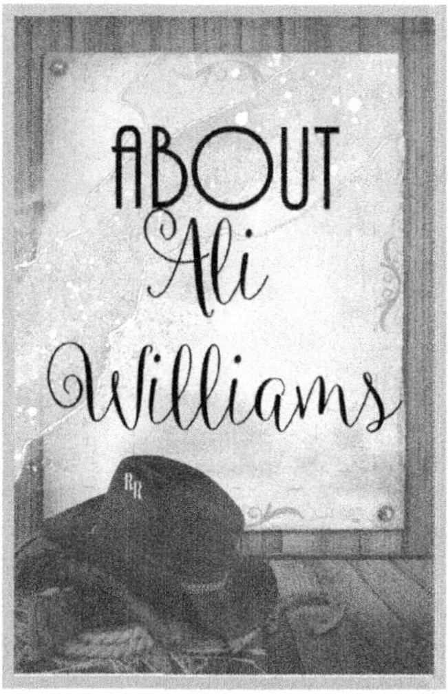

Ali Williams is a sapphic AuDHD author, editor and academic, who writes intensely kinky paranormals as Ali Williams, and fluffy and spicy age play romances as Ellie Rose.

Her PhD research focuses on the intersection between queerness and kink in feminist romance, and her sell-out online lecture series, Romancing the Discourse, discussed everything from how erotic romances use kink as liberation, to how paranormal romance can degender agency.

When she's not writing, she can invariably be found reading tarot, traipsing round the South Downs with her girlfriend, or playing boardgames with her queer, kinky found family.

Join Ali's Facebook group: The Shenanigan Squad, find her on Facebook https://bit.ly/46G3Bu6 and sign up to her Newsletter: https://bit.ly/3WVf6uf!

Tucked in the countryside with her family and numerous stuffies, Allie Belle writes the stories she has always wanted to read. She loves the idea of being a Little to a strong, stern Daddy and explores the dynamic in every way she can.

When not writing, you can find her snuggled under her princess blanket with her kindle or watching trashy reality TV.

You can also find Allie here:

Facebook Reader Group:
facebook.com/groups/allieaddysecret
Facebook Reader Group 2:
facebook.com/groups/
shenanigansquadreadergroup
E-mail: authoralliebelle@gmail.com

x.com/CLAficionado
instagram.com/claficionado
tiktok.com/@claficionado

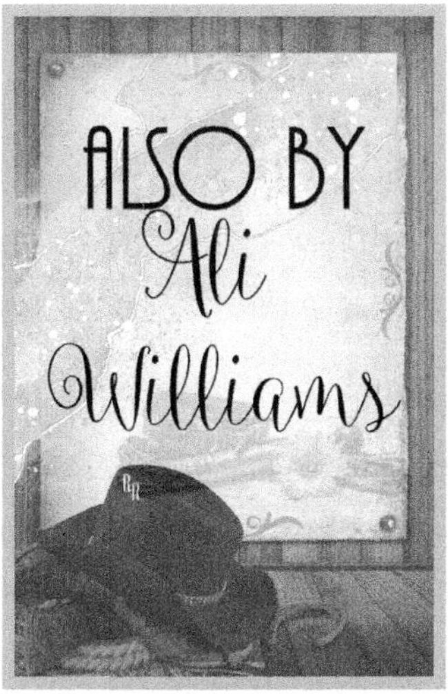

Rawhide Ranch Linked Books

Mandi's Little Mother's Day (Mandi and Amelia's book)

Writing as Ellie Rose

Kink the Halls (Riley and Wendy's story)

Erotic Romance

The Softest Kinksters Collection: An Erotic Romance Collection

Godstouched Universe

The Golden Apple Club Duology

The Apples Hung like Stars (Clíodhna and Janet)

Their Fruits like Honey (Aoibheall and Lizzie)

Where Goddesses Hunt

Lure Me to the Deep (Lí Ban and Niamh)

Chase Me in the Woods (The Morrígan and Ciara)

Catch Me in the Dark (Maeve and Eimear)

The Freed Hunt

Forged in Flames: A Dragon Shifter Romance

Value in Visions: A Sapphic Psychic Romance

Married in Moonlight: A Sapphic Psychic Wedding

The Arun Nixes

Nix and Tell: A Sapphic Fae Romance

Never Nix Up: A Sapphic Fae Romance

Don't Give a Nix: A Sapphic Fae Romance

Stuffie Hospital (writing as Ellie Rose)

A Little's Unicorn (Lillie and Aiden's book)

A Little's Reindeer (Georgie and Warren's book)

A Little's Lion (Kacie and Dex's book)

A Little's Patchwork Bear (Ralphie and Nate's book)

A Little's Witchy Bear (Rylie and Eve's book)

A Little's Monster (Christie and Dana's book)

A Little's Dino (Archie and Rebecca's book)

A Little's Elephant (Frankie and Grey's book)

A Little's Owl (Darcie and Richard's book)

A Little's Pegasus (Beanie and Abigail's book)

A Little's Christmas Wedding (Ralphie and Nate's wedding)

Stuffie Hospital London (writing as Ellie Rose)

A London Little's Llama (Billie and Mark's book)

A London Little's Moo (Tillie and Alex's book)

A London Little's Dragon (Jamie and Marian's book)

A London Little's Giraffe (Mossie and Daniel's book)

A London Little's Penguin (Rubie and Anna's book)

A London Little's Pom Pom (Rosie and Eloise's book)

A London Little's Bunny (Essie and Ben's book)

A London Little's Octopus (Charlie and Leon's book)

A London Little's Tiger (Susie and Briana's book)

The Littles' Market by the Sea (Writing as Ellie Rose)

Isla (Isla and Rachel's book)

Emma (Emma and Bryn's book)

Liv (Liv and Cat's book)

Sage (Sage and Lily's book)

Tess (Tess and Willow's book)

Reba (Reba and Kirby's book)

Nicole (Nicole and Violet's book)

Brooke (Brooke and Jenny's book)

Morgan (Morgan and Rose's book)

Wyn (Wyn and Tel's book)

River (River and Alice's book)

Aubrey (Aubrey and Helen's book)

Skylar (Skylar and Gabrielle's book)

Printed in Great Britain
by Amazon

59018062R00108